As the car climbed a s... ocean, Joe checked his map. Sachin seemed to be driving Frank and him in the opposite direction of the palace where the movie production was based. Then Sachin pulled over and stopped. From his window Joe could see waves far below, beating against a rocky cliff. "What are we stopping for?" he asked.

Sachin didn't answer. Instead, he jumped out of the car, ran around to the front, and gave it a powerful shove.

"Hey, we're rolling backward," Joe said.

Sachin peered in Frank's window as the car started to pick up speed. "Welcome to Bombay, boys," he said.

Frank grabbed for the man, but Sachin jumped back and darted away.

"Frank, my door's jammed," Joe said, rattling the handle.

Frank tried his. It was jammed, too.

"This is it," Joe shouted. "We're going over the cliff!"

Books in THE HARDY BOYS CASEFILES™ Series

THE HARDY BOYS

CASEFILES™

NO. 116

ACTING UP

FRANKLIN W. DIXON

AN ARCHWAY PAPERBACK
Published by POCKET BOOKS
New York London Toronto Sydney Tokyo Singapore

AN ARCHWAY PAPERBACK *Original*

An Archway Paperback published by
POCKET BOOKS, a division of Simon & Schuster Inc.
1230 Avenue of the Americas, New York, NY 10020

Copyright © 1996 by Simon & Schuster Inc.
Produced by Mega-Books of New York, Inc.

ISBN: 0-671-50488-6

First Archway Paperback printing October 1996

10 9 8 7 6 5 4 3 2 1

THE HARDY BOYS, AN ARCHWAY PAPERBACK and colophon are registered trademarks of Simon & Schuster Inc.

THE HARDY BOYS CASEFILES is a trademark of Simon & Schuster Inc.

Printed in the U.S.A.

IL 6+

ACTING UP

Chapter

1

JOE HARDY HELD OUT the video camera at arm's length and aimed it at his face. It was a new model, with a small color screen attached to the side. He watched himself run his free hand through his blond hair, as if he were a reporter getting ready to go on the air.

He pushed the Record button. "It's four in the morning here in India, and Frank and I have just landed at Bombay's Sahar International Airport," he said.

"Come on, Joe," Frank said to his younger brother. He was already striding toward the immigration counter.

"What's the rush?" Joe asked. He turned the camera on Frank as they walked. Frank's six-

1

foot-one frame was only about an inch high in the tiny screen.

"Rajiv Kapoor told Dad he'd have a car waiting for us," Frank said.

"That was before our two-hour delay in London," Joe said. "But I guess the car would wait until we got here."

Ahead, the jumble of passengers began to separate into several lines, and they picked what looked like the shortest one.

"It sure is crowded here in Bombay," Joe said, panning the camera to capture the colorful scene.

Frank had a thick file tucked under his arm and he jammed it under Joe's ribs, as if he were handing off a football. "Put the camera away and read this again while we're waiting," he said.

"I read every word of it already," Joe complained. He opened the file, though, and flipped through its contents. It was filled with information about Rajiv Kapoor, one of Bombay's internationally best-known film directors, and the man who was sending the car to meet them. Rajiv had met Fenton Hardy, Frank and Joe's father, at a film festival in New York several years earlier. Fenton had been in charge of security.

After a three-year hiatus, Rajiv was making a new movie. The project was so top secret that no one in the rumor-ridden Bombay film business even knew its title. Lately a number of accidents had led Rajiv to believe that someone was sabotaging his production. Wanting to maintain secrecy, he'd asked Fenton to come to Bombay and investigate. The local police couldn't be trusted, Rajiv had said. They would sell information to the press. Fenton was working on another urgent investigation, so he had asked his sons to go in his place.

As the line advanced, Joe reviewed the facts concerning Bombay's film industry. "Bollywood" was supposed to be just as glamorous and exciting as Hollywood and produced around 175 films a year. Many of the Indian blockbusters were action-adventure stories with a bit of romance, singing, and dancing thrown in. Joe figured he could live without the singing and dancing, but he was looking forward to the elaborate sets and wild stunts.

"Your passport, sir?"

Joe looked up to see an immigration officer eyeing him impatiently. After the officer stamped each of the boys' passports, Frank and Joe moved on to an extremely crowded baggage carousel.

"Tough crowd," Frank said, craning his neck as he searched for their bags.

Joe held up a letter from the file. "Did you make a note of this? Where Rajiv wrote to Dad that he had writer's block after his last film."

"No wonder he's anxious," Frank said.

The plan was to have the brothers pose as interns from a film school in New York. They'd work as production assistants on the set, which would give them full access to the crew and actors.

"Rajiv gets involved in every aspect of his films, all the details from casting to writing and directing," Joe said.

"Maybe he's just a control freak," Frank said. "Those incidents he described to Dad—lightbulbs blowing out, the emergency generator failing—all sound pretty mild to me."

"What about his assistant getting beaten up?" Joe asked.

"It could have just been a mugging."

"No way Dad would let us miss school if he thought Rajiv was only overreacting," Joe said. "I guess we'll find out soon enough, though." Over the shoulders of the crowd he spotted their duffel bags and, using his running back's build, wove through the knot of people to snag them off the conveyor belt.

The Hardys hurried to customs, where there was an even longer wait than at immigration, unfortunately. The officials seemed determined to search just about everyone's bags. Obviously, there were a lot of people bringing in undeclared goods. The woman in front of them had a VCR wrapped in an old sari. She was forced to unpack her two other cases, revealing an expensive camera and a mini tape recorder, for which she'd be charged duty.

Finally the Hardys' turn came. They were asked to show the luggage tags on their tickets to verify that they matched the tags on their bags. Then, after a brief search, they were free to leave.

An ocean breeze wafted through the double doors of the arrivals lounge. Although it was five-thirty in the morning, it was still dark outside. Frank caught a glimpse of palm trees in the middle of the driveway silhouetted against the dark sky. Rajiv had said his assistant, Sachin, would be waiting for them with a sign that read Hardy. The Hardys glanced at the people holding up names written on scraps of cardboard or paper, but they couldn't find theirs.

"He's probably out in the car—asleep," Joe said as they stepped outside. The air was balmy. Cars and taxis blocked the loading zone as people hugged their relatives and loaded bags into every available space in and on the vehicles.

Joe jumped as the outdoor speakers of the public address system crackled with static. A booming voice speaking in Hindi drowned out the murmur of people greeting one another. Armored Jeeps and police cars, lights flashing and sirens blaring, pulled into the drive and screeched to a halt, blocking traffic on all sides.

Joe glanced at Frank. "I wonder what's going on."

Security guards carrying guns and batons jumped from their Jeeps and began herding everyone back onto the loading zone. When the voice on the P.A. system switched to English, Joe heard something about explosives, but the wailing sirens drowned out the rest.

"Hey, watch it," Frank heard Joe say, as the unruly crowd jostled them out into the street. As he looked in the direction of Joe's voice, he saw his brother swept aside by a group of German tourists.

"Joe!" he called as he was pushed in the opposite direction. A woman carrying a small child wrapped in a blanket elbowed him out of the way. A police officer started arguing with a balding man who was trying to push through the crowd with an overloaded baggage cart.

"Someone will take my bags if I leave them," the man exclaimed.

"No one is leaving the airport right now, including you!" The officer used his short-barreled riot shotgun to block the man's path.

Frank stopped another officer who was hurrying by. "What's happening?"

The man frowned. "You came in on the flight from London?"

"Yes."

"You must wait here until you are instructed to go back inside to have your bags rechecked," he said curtly. A few minutes later he herded Frank and other passengers back into the arrivals lounge.

A customs official checked Frank's bag even more carefully this time, unfolding his shirts and jeans and feeling around for hidden compartments. Frank asked what was going on, but the official wouldn't even raise his head until he was satisfied that there was nothing suspicious in Frank's luggage. Finally, he zipped Frank's duffel and handed it back. "We received a warning that someone was bringing in explosives on the flight from London," he said. "Is anyone traveling with you?"

"My brother, Joe. We got separated outside."

"He's left the airport?" The official studied Frank suspiciously.

"I don't think so."

The man picked up the phone and made a call. The only thing he said in English was Joe's name. As the official was finishing his call, Frank heard a familiar voice say, "I'm back." He turned to see Joe beside him, out of breath.

"Where were you?" Frank asked. "This guy thought you'd left the airport."

"Yeah, sure, I found our ride and decided to leave you here," Joe said with a smile. "Seriously, I ran into Sachin. He said he called ahead and found out our plane was delayed, so he just got here. They made him park outside the airport and walk in. Security isn't letting any cars in now."

Joe handed over his bag and video camera for inspection, after which they were allowed to leave. Back out in the loading zone, they watched as the sun rose. A slightly fishy smell of the ocean hung in the early morning mist.

Frank was looking forward to a shower and change of clothes. They had only two weeks here, and he hoped they could wrap up the case quickly and still see some of the city before heading back to Bayport. That would make all the cramming for the midterms they'd had to take before leaving worthwhile.

"Sachin said he was here yesterday to pick up Vijay Tate," Joe said. Vijay, the star of the movie, had been in London, visiting his uncle, Biku Tate, who was Rajiv's producer and main investor.

"There he is." Joe pointed to a heavily bearded man with a dark red turban. He was wearing mirrored sunglasses, black pants, and a loose-fitting red tunic that matched his turban.

Spotting them, Sachin nodded at Joe, who introduced Frank. "So you've come to Bombay to learn how we make movies, eh?" Sachin said. "Maybe you bring good luck with you. We could use some."

Frank thought he saw Sachin crack a smile, but he couldn't be sure because of the beard. "Let's hope so," he replied, not wanting to sound too curious. "We heard you may be jinxed." They walked past a terminal that was under construction, its scaffolding hanging out over them, and then turned onto what looked like a major street.

"That's the car?" Frank asked. It was tiny, with a chassis not much bigger than that of a golf cart. "How are we supposed to fit into that?"

Joe was surprised, too. He'd been expecting a stretch limo or at least a European luxury sedan.

"We'll put your bags in the front seat next to me," Sachin said, taking the two duffel bags from the boys and squashing them in the narrow front seat. "The boot is too small."

Frank and Joe squeezed into the backseat, their knees almost up to their chins. Between the luggage and Sachin's turban, they could barely see out the windshield.

Joe had almost forgotten that in India they drove on the left side of the road, as they do in Britain. That also explained why they used the British word *boot* for trunk. Determined to see something of the city, he and Frank rolled down their grimy windows, which went only halfway.

Sachin drove like a maniac, zipping the tiny car through the maze of narrow streets, switching lanes on a whim all the while honking at pedestrians and bicyclists. Swinging around a corner, they had to swerve to miss a wooden cart being pulled by a fat, lumbering water buffalo and nearly skidded into a teetering double-decker bus packed with people. The smell of diesel fumes came in through the open windows, and Frank had to grip the door frame to stay in his seat. He was having a hard time enjoying the sights.

"How far is the set?" Frank asked after a while. The streets had changed and were no longer narrow and crowded. They climbed a steep grade, leaving the city behind and rising high above the ocean.

Joe checked his map. They seemed to be driving southeast, in the opposite direction of the palace where the production was based. He was about to ask where they were headed when Sachin pulled over and stopped. From his window Joe could see waves far below, beating against a rocky cliff. "What are we stopping for?" he asked.

Sachin didn't answer. Instead, he jumped out of the car, ran around to the front, and gave it a powerful shove.

"Hey, we're rolling backward," Joe said.

Sachin peered in Frank's window as the car started to pick up speed. "Welcome to Bombay, boys," he said.

Frank could see his own distorted reflection in Sachin's sunglasses. He grabbed for the man, but Sachin jumped back and darted away.

"Frank, my door's jammed," Joe said, rattling the handle. Frank tried his. It was jammed, too.

"This is it," Joe shouted. "We're going over the cliff!"

Chapter

2

THEY COULD HEAR AND FEEL the crunch of tires on gravel as the car picked up momentum. Joe tried to reach over the front seat to get to the brakes, but there wasn't enough room.

Frank cocked his right arm and smashed his elbow into the half-open window next to him. The glass shattered, and he hurled himself through, rolling away from the car as he hit the ground. He turned to look for his brother.

The car looked as if it was going over as Joe flew through the window and dropped to the ground, skidding on the gravel and stopping just inches from the cliff edge.

The little orange automobile balanced on the rim, stuck on some jagged rocks, its rear axle hanging over a hundred-foot drop.

"Are you okay?" Joe heard Frank's voice behind him.

Joe stood up and peered over the cliff. "Just great," he said, brushing off his jeans and checking for cuts. "Stay back while I get our bags." Joe approached the car gingerly. He had to lean out over the cliff to reach the passenger door handle. He opened the door slowly with his left hand and grasped the bags with his right. He made sure he was clear of the car before yanking the bags out. The car teetered, then went over, falling toward the rocks in what looked like slow motion. Joe winced at the wrenching sound of the impact.

He turned back to Frank. "I wonder what Rajiv is going to say when we tell him his trusted assistant tried to kill us."

"I think we can assume that wasn't Sachin," Frank replied. "Look at this." He held up a fake beard and mustache. "This came off in my hand when I grabbed for the guy."

They shouldered their bags and started walking back toward the city to find a cab. Off to the right, the Arabian Sea stretched out gray and flat as far as they could see. In all other directions Bombay sprawled, its densely packed tenements and high-rises swimming in a smoggy haze.

"Why would someone try to kill us?" Joe wondered. "Dad said that not even Biku Tate would know the real reason we're here. As far as everyone is concerned, we're just a couple of interns."

They came to a busy intersection, and Frank hailed a cab. This time they made sure the driver took them in the right direction, toward the Worli Sea Face, north of the center of the city.

"Our fake Sachin wasn't just some unscrupulous cabdriver," Frank said. "He knew too much about us. That probably means someone on the set knows who we are."

"It also means Rajiv probably isn't just being paranoid about somebody trying to sabotage his film," Joe said.

The cab dropped the Hardys at the set, an old palace belonging to a distant relative of Rajiv.

"It must be nice to be related to the Maharaja of Rajghar," Joe said, staring up at the enormous white stone compound. The palace stood in sharp contrast to a brick textile factory across the street. Many of the factory's windows were broken and immediately surrounding the factory was nothing but a shantytown. People were living right out on the sidewalk, cooking their breakfasts on small, rusted grills, hanging clothes out to dry on lines strung between telephone poles.

Frank and Joe walked around and entered the palace through a door in the back. The place looked like a fort with its crenelated walls. A guard, stationed in a small booth near the door, checked their identification before letting them in.

Joe let out a low whistle. "This is like stepping through a time warp," he said.

The courtyard was immaculately landscaped, with paved paths and carefully tended flowerbeds. The Hardys walked toward a two-story stone structure with massive columns and arches along the length of it.

Another guard rechecked their names against a list on a clipboard and let them in the building through a high iron double door that looked like an elaborate armoire.

"Look, Frank," Joe said as they walked in. Above the intricately carved doorway were two black elephant statues, facing each other so that their raised trunks were nearly touching. The elephants had gold blankets painted over the bulk of their bodies, and their features were painted in white and yellow. The paint had faded and chipped over the centuries, but they were still striking.

The inside courtyard had a tile mosaic floor and several doorways leading off it. There were two men in the middle, engaged in a frantic conversation. The older one caught sight of the Hardys and stopped talking.

"Hi," Frank said. "We're looking for Rajiv Kapoor."

"Are you Frank and Joe Hardy?"

The man crossed the courtyard and introduced himself as Kapoor. He was tall, with gray hair down to his shoulders, and he wore sandals and baggy white pants with a matching tunic. He wore a linen vest over the tunic and carried a clipboard in his left hand. Though his voice was jovial, his bushy eyebrows came together in a frown as he checked out the Hardys.

"Where have you been?" he asked. With his slightly hooked nose, he looked like an angry eagle. "Sachin said he looked everywhere." He indicated the young man behind him. "He just returned from the airport."

Frank and Joe's suspicions were confirmed. The man Rajiv was pointing to looked nothing like the man who'd picked them up. Sachin was a thin, wiry man dressed in jeans, sandals, and a crisp cotton shirt. He had a well-trimmed beard and mustache and wore round glasses that made him look more like a college instructor than a director's assistant.

Frank and Joe had decided to brief Rajiv in private, so they said nothing about the Sachin impostor. "Someone was supposedly smuggling explosives into the airport," Frank explained. "It was pretty chaotic, so we figured Sachin never made it through the police barricade."

"Explosives?" Rajiv turned to Sachin. "You never told me about that."

"I was just getting to that part of the story," Sachin said evenly. He turned to the boys. "I'm very sorry about this. When I finally got into the airport, it was so late that I figured you must have given up on me."

"Well, Sachin, just make sure nothing like this happens again," Rajiv said. "This is their first trip to Bombay, and we wouldn't want them to have a bad impression, would we?"

Excusing himself, Rajiv went into one of the rooms off the courtyard.

Sachin motioned for Frank and Joe to put their bags down. "Don't worry," he said, grinning. "He tends to overreact when things don't go according to plan."

"Is the production on schedule?" Frank asked as they followed Sachin down a long marble-paved gallery.

"Barely," Sachin said. "We've had a couple of problems in the last three weeks that have delayed us considerably." He pointed up to the high ceiling, where some frayed ropes hung. "Two weeks ago the chandelier that belongs here came crashing down. It was made of wood and iron, very heavy. Luckily no one was hurt.

"There was a bad case of food poisoning among the crew, which isn't unusual in the tropics but a nuisance nonetheless. The electricity has gone out a couple of times. The guard claims to have seen a ghost in the corridors, but I don't think a ghost did this." He pointed to a faded bruise on his forehead.

"How did that happen?" Frank asked.

"I was leaving the set, locking up after everyone had gone home late one night. The guard was nowhere around, so I thought he had fallen asleep or gone to get something to eat."

"How many guards patrol at night?" Joe asked.

"Just one," Sachin answered. "It was very dark. The street outside the palace is not lit at night. I had my flashlight under my chin as I locked the gate. When I heard rustling noises in the jasmine, I called out, but no one answered. Suddenly I felt a hand pulling my head back. My flashlight fell, and the next thing I knew someone was punching me in the stomach and then ramming my head into the iron gate. I tried to fight, but there were two of them, and finally I passed out."

"Did you get a look at them?"

Sachin shook his head. "And they didn't say a word. Once I was on the ground, they ran off."

"Do you think it has anything to do with the film?" Joe asked.

Sachin shrugged. "Those men were probably only looking for some fun, though a lot of people in town do resent Rajiv's way of doing business."

"Why? Doesn't he play by the rules?" Frank asked.

"Actors here like to work on several films at once," Sachin said. "I've heard of people being involved in as many as fourteen different projects, but Rajiv forces his actors to sign exclusive eight-week contracts. During that time they are not allowed to work on any other productions."

"Two months isn't much time to shoot a film," Frank noted.

"Especially since the average shoot here takes three years," Sachin said. "You can see how the pressure is building. If Rajiv doesn't deliver the film by the end of the year, he'll lose his backing, not only from Biku but from the foreign investors Biku has assembled."

Something didn't make sense to Joe. "Why would actors agree to exclusive contracts?" he asked.

"Vijay and Kamala are both rising stars," Sachin said. "Rajiv hasn't done a film in three years, and they were willing to sign exclusives to get the chance to work with him. Once they were signed on, confidence in the project grew and more actors and crew members signed exclusives also. Now, with all the problems we're having, people are getting nervous."

Sachin led Frank and Joe down a narrow corridor with gilded walls and latticed stone screens.

"Take a look, Joe," Frank said. "You can see down into the courtyard from here."

"The women of the royal family could look through these screens without being seen," Sachin explained. "You'll see these throughout the palace.

"Frank," Sachin continued, "you have been assigned to work with the production manager, Mahesh Bhatt, for the time being. Joe, you'll work with the lighting crew for now."

At the end of the corridor, Sachin directed Frank to Mahesh's office, located at the back of the prop and set design room, and then left with Joe for the Hall of Public Audiences, where most of the interior scenes were being shot.

Frank entered a well-lit room. The floor was covered with a piece of brown tarp to protect the marble, but that didn't take away from the splendor of the arched windows and painted walls. At the back of the room was an eight-panel wooden screen, carved with a line of elephants, each using its trunk to grasp the tail of the one in front of it.

Frank heard scuffling behind the screen, followed by a loud yelp of pain. "Aieee!"

Then came a swishing sound and more scuffling. Frank rushed around the screen to find a man trapped against the wall, covering his face with his arms as another man charged at him with a sword.

Frank lunged for the attacker, knocking him over and grabbing his wrist. The sword clattered to the floor, but the man Frank had just rescued grabbed it and turned on him. He wielded the big weapon in his right hand, backed Frank up against the wall and, with a determined grimace, swung it in a deadly arc straight at Frank's head.

Chapter

3

FRANK DUCKED and the sword sliced through the air so close to his cheek that he could feel the wind. The man brandished the weapon, then swung the tip of the blade around, holding it against Frank's chest. The polished steel gleamed white in the lights.

"Had you scared, yes?" the man said, and broke into a grin. He held out his hand and helped Frank up. The other man shook with laughter.

"I'm Mahesh, the production manager," said Frank's attacker. "You must be one of the American interns. This clown is Alok, the stunt coordinator."

Alok couldn't stop laughing. He took the sword from Mahesh and ran his thumb along the blade, testing its edge. "Just a prop, see? Mahesh and I were staging one of the scenes I worked out." He was tall and muscular compared to Mahesh, who was older and slouched a bit. Mahesh was clean-shaven, while Alok had a mustache and heavy sideburns.

Frank shook his head. "It looked pretty real to me."

"That's the point," Mahesh said. "If we couldn't fool you, who could we fool?"

"So there's fighting in this movie?" Frank asked, trying to hide his embarrassment. "Sachin told us it wasn't a typical Bollywood production."

Mahesh rolled his eyes. "I'll say. This is a very serious picture, no singing and dancing. We're lucky they didn't take out all the action scenes as well."

"But it's still a good story," Alok said.

"That's what I heard," Frank said. "Maybe you could fill me in on the details."

"What do you know?" Mahesh asked.

"Just that it's based on a true story about this guru, Ram something."

"Ram Jagannath," Alok said. "Ten years ago he was one of the most popular spiritual teachers. He set up an ashram in an old palace like this one. He had very loyal followers."

"So it was some kind of cult?" Frank asked.

"Nothing quite so obvious," Mahesh said, leading Frank out into the vast prop and set design room. "People came and went as they pleased.

In fact, a lot of film people would go there just to spend a few days in quiet meditation. Apparently the ashram was very peaceful. Until Ram was caught smuggling explosives and selling them to the highest bidder. He even had a rival ashram bombed, and several people were killed."

"That doesn't sound too spiritual to me," Frank said.

"That's not the strangest part of the story." Alok put the sword back in its scabbard and placed it on a shelf crowded with props.

"After his arrest," Mahesh went on, "the police discovered that Ram Jagannath was an Englishman posing as an Indian."

Frank couldn't believe it. "What? Didn't anyone notice?"

"He claimed to be an Indian raised and educated in England," Alok said as he started to choreograph a fight scene. He talked as he went through the motions of two men grappling. "He said he'd returned to India when he got sick of the Western way of living."

"I guess he figured people were more likely to trust an Indian guru than an Englishman," Frank said.

"Absolutely," Mahesh said. "He pulled it off, too. He had thick black hair and a long black beard that covered most of his face. He spoke Hindi the way foreign-raised Indians speak it, and because there were so many foreigners in his flock, he spoke English in his public addresses, anyway. People loved his deep, booming voice," Mahesh added. "Or so I've heard. I never actually saw him. Did you, Alok?"

Alok shook his head. He moved nimbly and powerfully from one wrestling move to another, shooting down low to throw an imaginary foe. "I only know what I read," Alok said. "A couple of his disciples tried to break him out of jail one night. He was shot dead, and they escaped."

"However," Mahesh said, "Rajiv's story doesn't focus on Jagannath as much as on a couple of people who meet at his ashram, fall in love, and then find they are caught in the middle of a corrupt and dangerous situation."

"Was anyone arrested after the escape attempt?" Frank asked.

"No, they probably went up north and crossed the border into Pakistan," Mahesh said. "There's been no sign of them for years. In fact, the ashram was sold to a hotel chain. I doubt anyone except Rajiv remembers Jagannath and his groupies."

"This movie should change that," Frank said.

"We'll see," Mahesh said.

Frank noticed more wooden screens that partitioned the vast room into sections. In one section were long metal racks of costumes, in another was a marble counter running along a mirrored wall. Styrofoam wig blocks with wigs and mustaches of various styles lined the counter.

Frank helped Mahesh organize the costumes

and props for future scenes. As they worked, Frank found out that most of the crew arrived on the set by seven every morning. The fake Sachin had left them at the cliff at six-thirty, so he would have had plenty of time to make it to the set on time, Frank figured. That fact, combined with all the information the impostor knew about the Hardys, convinced Frank that he must be part of the cast or crew.

Meanwhile Joe was busy setting up lights in the big hall when Sachin called him over to meet a tall man with light brown hair and hazel eyes. "This is Nikhil, Vijay Tate's stand-in and best friend in the film."

Joe shook hands with Nikhil, who stood out among the dark-haired cast and crew.

"I heard you were delayed by a bomb scare this morning," Nikhil said. "How long did it take you to get out of the airport?"

"A while," Joe said. "It wasn't really a bomb scare, though. They said someone tried to bring in explosives."

Before he could ask any questions, the assistant director asked Nikhil to sit on a cushion on the floor, in front of the dais with Ram Jagannath's magisterial chair. He wanted to make sure that both the main camera and the secondary units were properly positioned to film two men and Jagannath.

"Joe," Rajiv called, "find out if Kamala's ready. As long as we're set up, we'll shoot the scene when Jagannath holds a private audience with her and the two boys."

Getting directions from one of the crew, Joe hurried along a corridor to the group of rooms put aside for the cast. Because the maharaja didn't want the gilded doors ruined with Scotch tape or glue, none of the dressing rooms were labeled. Kamala Devi, the heroine, had hung a glittery gold star with her name on it on her doorknob. Joe knocked and she answered, "Come in."

The actress was sitting at a dresser with her back to the door. Joe saw a beautiful young woman with wide gray eyes reflected in her mirror. Her black hair hung almost to the floor. She wore a nose ring and gold hoop earrings, and her long red fingernails tapped the dresser impatiently.

"You're not Minnie," she snapped.

"I'm Joe Hardy, one of the new interns."

Kamala turned around. "What do you want?"

"Rajiv wants to know if you're ready for the next scene. They're going to shoot it right after this one."

"Oh, pooh," she said. "What's the rush, then? You're American, aren't you? Why don't you take a seat and tell me all about Hollywood?"

Joe picked his way through several piles of clothing scattered on the floor and took a seat. However, before he could say anything, Kamala started complaining about the script.

"So," Joe said, "you feel this isn't a good project for you?"

Kamala backtracked. "Oh no, don't misunderstand. Working with Rajiv Kapoor is every actress's dream. But a movie with no singing and dancing—it seems so dull. I don't know how Rajiv is going to save it."

"Is that why he's being so secretive about the production?" Joe asked, watching her draw a thick black line along her eyelid.

"He doesn't want his big comeback jeopardized by unscrupulous gossips. He thinks the film could do well here, provided he's given a chance to show it before it's dismissed by critics."

"There's no market for serious movies?"

"The audience wants entertainment. They have certain expectations, and our job is to meet them. I thought Biku understood that."

She sounded bitter, but before Joe could ask her if she'd tried to get out of her contract, there was a knock at the door. Without waiting for an answer, a heavyset, light-skinned man, with a black handlebar mustache, stepped in. His round stomach wobbled slightly under his loose orange tunic and pants.

"Who are you?" he asked, frowning at Joe.

"Please, Tariq," Kamala admonished. "Where are your manners? This is Joe, one of our new American production assistants. Be nice to him or you won't get your cup of tea between takes."

"You must be Tariq Khan, the villain of the

story," Joe said. Joe knew he was the one who played Ram Jagannath.

Tariq eyed Joe suspiciously. "A villain only as Rajiv imagines him. Don't mistake this story for fact."

His voice was deep, with a British accent, but Joe was more curious about what Tariq had just said. Why did he sound so irritated about Rajiv's take on Jagannath?

"We're late," Tariq said, and left the room as abruptly as he'd entered it.

"Does he always come in to tell you when you're late?" Joe asked.

Kamala laughed. "He studied at the Royal Academy in London and talks and acts as if he were royalty. He even refers to himself as 'we.' Working in a palace and playing a guru has only made it worse. I'm afraid he takes the role far too seriously."

When Joe returned to the set, he found Frank there with Vijay Tate. Sachin introduced Joe to the star. Vijay looked a lot like Nikhil, although he was much darker. He had shaggy black hair and a thin nose. His dark eyes were ringed with circles of fatigue, and he wore a small gold hoop in his left ear. He was dressed in a plain beige robe for the ashram scene.

"You must be tired," he said to Joe and Frank. "I flew in yesterday and still had to sleep in this morning." He seemed unconcerned that he'd kept everyone waiting.

27

"Good thing you did arrive yesterday," Joe said. "You missed all the chaos at the airport."

Vijay nodded. "I was going to send Sachin there this afternoon to pick up one of my suitcases. It was left in London, and the airline called me to say it would be on today's flight."

"I should wait till later," Sachin said. "The airport will be crazy all day because of the confusion this morning." His cellular phone rang, and he was soon engrossed in a heated conversation.

"He's trying to find a snake charmer," Vijay translated for the Hardys.

"A real snake charmer?" Joe asked.

Vijay nodded. "Jagannath's ashram was on a huge estate, where he had all kinds of wildlife—tigers, peacocks, even an elephant. In the movie, he keeps a snake in a basket by his feet."

Joe watched as Sachin shut his phone with a shake of his head. "This is impossible to arrange. Why do we need a real snake, anyway? I have to talk Rajiv into something more practical." He disappeared down the corridor, muttering to himself.

Vijay and the Hardys chatted for a few minutes before getting back to work. Then while Joe helped the script supervisor by writing down the angles for lights and the placement of cameras, Frank headed back to Mahesh's office to get the storyboards for Rajiv.

Walking down the quiet corridor, Frank heard a squeak above him. He looked up. The vaulted corridor ceiling was at least twenty feet high, and there were balconies about halfway up, with more of the see-through stone screens.

Frank took a few more steps, then stopped. It sounded as though someone was shadowing him from the balcony above. He heard the squeak of a shoe on a waxed floor.

"Who's there?" he called.

No one answered. Frank continued walking to the end of the corridor. Someone *was* up there. Frank silently headed up a dark, narrow staircase to his right.

Shining his pocket flashlight up the worn spiral stairs, he braced himself with one hand and crept up. At the top he saw tiny shafts of light shining in through the screens. He cast his flashlight beam across the balcony, but it was just a dark, empty space.

He heard another squeak coming from his left and shone his light in that direction, but there was nothing there either.

Then a voice behind him said, "Stop, no one is allowed up here."

Frank started to wheel around and felt something crash down on the back of his head so hard his teeth clacked together. The dappled light through the screens swirled in his eyes, then everything went black.

Chapter

4

FRANK WOKE UP to find a man with a pencil-thin mustache and watery brown eyes that fluttered anxiously staring down at him. It was the guard.

"What happened?" Frank asked. He was back downstairs in the hallway. He had a headache, but nothing felt broken. He sat up slowly, but his head started spinning, so he lay back down on the cold marble. "The last thing I remember was someone saying that no one is allowed up in the balcony."

"That was him," Joe said, jerking his thumb at the guard. "He heard you walking around up there and went to tell you to come down. He says he got there just as a ghost attacked you. He's pretty freaked out."

"That was no ghost." Frank's vision cleared, and with Joe's help, he managed to stand up.

Sachin came down the hall with a doctor, speaking as he walked. "What were you doing up there?"

Frank rubbed the back of his head. "I heard someone, so I thought I'd check it out."

"Oh, we may have a real problem, then," Sachin said. "I think someone was sent to spy on the production—probably by Alex Chandraswamy."

"Maybe it was just a reporter or something," Joe said. He didn't want Sachin alerting everyone on the set and driving their saboteur underground.

"No matter," Sachin said. "That would be almost as bad."

The doctor checked the bruise on Frank's head, then flashed his penlight in each of Frank's eyes. "I pronounce you *A-okay*. Take it easy this afternoon and get some rest. You should be just fine."

"Thanks," Frank said. He turned to Sachin. "Who is this Alex Chantingswamy?"

"Chandraswamy," he said, correcting Frank. "He's another director. Alex and Rajiv have a long history of bad blood. I don't have any idea how it started. From now on, the two of you should not talk to anyone you don't know. We have to be careful." Sachin turned abruptly and led the doctor back down the hall.

Joe and Frank questioned the guard, who was still shaken up. He couldn't add anything to Frank's version of the story. He'd heard the sound of Frank's getting hit and falling to the ground, then the squeaking noises he swore were the footsteps of a ghost.

The Hardys walked back to the set. "Mahesh told me there are about sixty crew and seventy-five actors and extras, male and female," Frank said. "That's a lot of people to keep track of."

They didn't get a chance to talk further. Frank rested on a pile of pillows in a corner of the Hall of Audiences while Joe went back to work with the script supervisor. They had Nikhil and other stand-ins walk through the action while Rajiv shouted orders and suggestions from his director's chair. At five they broke for afternoon tea, and finally, after eleven takes of one scene, Rajiv decided to call it a day.

Sachin drove the Hardys to Rajiv's house in Malabar Hill, one of Bombay's most exclusive neighborhoods. The house had a plush grassy lawn and a circular driveway that came right up to the thick columns of the front porch. The top of the porch was a railed balcony that could be reached through glass double doors on the second floor. Sachin led Frank and Joe to their room. "Dinner will be ready in an hour," he said, and closed the door as he left.

"This room is big enough for a game of half-court basketball," Joe said. From the wide windows he could clearly see the border between city and sea. The densely packed yellow lights of Bombay reached out to a certain point, then stopped, met by the vast, black space of ocean.

Every few seconds a red light blinked far out to sea.

While he unpacked, Frank told Joe about meeting Mahesh and Alok. "Mahesh told me that crew members work as freelancers. They like to work on lots of productions at once, too, just like the actors. These fourteen-hour days aren't giving them a chance to work anywhere else."

"Maybe a lot of people are unhappy with Rajiv right now," Joe said, "and want to get out of their contracts."

"Or maybe Sachin's right. Someone's working for one of Rajiv's rivals." Frank took the fake beard out of his bag to examine it again. It was a very distinct color, shiny black with a few streaks of gray and maybe even some dark red. He handed it to Joe.

"It feels really coarse," Joe said. "Like animal hair."

"It's our only clue so far." Frank opened the windows and stretched out on his bed. He noticed that there was a statue of the Hindi deity Vishnu on his nightstand. "Hey, Joe, doesn't this statue look kind of like that lead actress—Kamala, I think her name is?"

"I guess." Joe was still studying the beard. "Speaking of Kamala, I think she's worried the movie's going to flop and ruin her career."

"Is she trying to get out of her contract?"

"I didn't get a chance to ask her." Joe picked a sock out of his duffel bag and stuffed the beard inside it for safekeeping. "Tariq interrupted us, but he had a few interesting things to say about Ram Jagannath. Tariq seems to be a big fan of the guru."

"I wonder why," Frank said with a yawn. He was starting to fall asleep just as Sachin knocked and stuck his head in the doorway, his thin neck making him appear to be a bird.

"It is time to come down for dinner," he said, and disappeared.

When they got downstairs, the Hardys saw that Rajiv had planned a working dinner with senior members of the crew and cast. Vijay had changed into an expensive-looking gray suit and sat at the beautifully polished mahogany dining table, talking amiably to Alok and Mahesh.

"Now we can really get to know each other," Vijay said, standing to shake hands with both the Hardys. "How's your head?"

"Still sore," Frank admitted.

"That guard is overworked," Mahesh said. "He has strict orders to keep the press off the premises, and he also has to watch us carefully and make sure that we leave the place exactly as we found it. We'd have an easier time with security if we were using a studio."

"But we'd be paying thousands of rupees to build a palace interior," Rajiv said as he entered the room. "Watching out for priceless possessions that have been in my family for generations is a smaller price to pay, don't you think?"

34

Mahesh muttered something under his breath.

"Yes, yes, Mahesh," Rajiv said. "You've told me a thousand times how impossible this whole thing is."

"When we unionize," Mahesh said, "you won't be able to get away with making us work these hours."

Rajiv seemed to ignore Mahesh's comment. "Come now," he said, "we have a meal to eat. Ramlal has prepared a special South Indian dinner."

Sachin came in, followed by the servant, Ramlal, who was dressed in baggy white pants and a white pullover shirt that looked like doctors' scrubs. He passed around steaming bowls of *sambar*, a lentil soup with bits of vegetable in it, and small dishes of coconut chutney.

Joe tried to hide his disappointment. He was hungry. Somehow a bowl of soup and coconut chutney didn't seem like it would be enough. Next Ramlal came around with huge crepelike pancakes filled with curried potatoes.

"*Masala dosa,*" Sachin explained, showing Joe how to break off pieces of the crisp pancake with his fingers and then dip them into the *sambar*.

Relieved by the sight of more food, Joe began eating. The masala dosa and sambar turned out to be the appetizer, which was followed by rice and spicy vegetables, then fresh yogurt. Dessert was mango ice cream.

The Hardys were anxious to talk to Rajiv

alone. After their long flight, big meal, and day on the set, the Hardys pleaded jet lag when Sachin suggested a drive around the city for a nighttime tour.

"No tour," Rajiv said. "I need to talk to Frank and Joe about their responsibilities. And I want to meet with each of you separately about tomorrow's shoot."

Leaving Alok, Mahesh, and Vijay to watch an old Hindi film, Frank and Joe followed Rajiv into his study.

The room was lined with bookcases stacked with leather-bound screenplays. Rajiv's desk faced the door and had legs that turned into eagle talons holding balls at the floor. Two comfortable office chairs faced the paper-strewn desk. They all sat down, and Frank and Joe quickly filled Rajiv in on their ride from the airport.

"Your description of the driver sounds as if he could be almost anyone I know," Rajiv said. "I don't understand—no one is supposed to know why you're here except me."

"Well," Joe said, "it just so happens that the guy knew exactly who we were and what he planned to do with us."

Frank saw that Joe was losing his cool, so he changed the subject. "Have you noticed any pattern to the incidents on the set?" he asked.

Rajiv sighed. "At first I told myself it was just bad luck when the lights failed or the emergency generator didn't come on. These were nothing dangerous. But a week after these incidents, some members of the crew got violently ill after eating lunch at the palace. Not all of us got sick, and the doctor told me that some kind of herbal poison had been put in their food. How, I don't know, but ten people had to be hospitalized. Then Sachin got beaten up, and I decided to call your father."

"How do you know he wasn't just mugged?" Frank asked.

"They didn't take his money. They weren't even interested in his copy of the script, which I'm sure they could've sold to the press."

"Sachin certainly is worried about the press," Joe said.

"That's right," Frank added. "And he's also uptight about someone named Alex Chandraswamy."

"Ah, yes." Rajiv nodded his head. "I was going to tell you about Alex. Of all my enemies—and one makes many in this business—he hates me the most. We were friends, but I had to take over a project of his more than twenty years ago. The producer fired him, and when I stepped in as director, he claimed I'd stabbed him in the back."

"So he would love to see this project fail," Frank said.

"Yes." Rajiv dug around in the papers on his desk. "He's been holding a grudge for all these years, even though he's now very successful on his own. In fact, there's a big party planned for the opening of his new movie. Sachin told me the guest list reads like a who's who of Bollywood."

"I'd like to have an invitation to that party," Joe said. He imagined meeting a few more beautiful leading ladies like Kamala—not to mention widening the scope of their investigation. "Maybe we could ask around to see if we can dig anything up."

Rajiv finally fished two sets of keys from the stacks of papers and books. "I'm sure I can arrange that," he said. "I wanted to give you these, too. They're keys to two mopeds in my garage, should you need to get around when Sachin is busy."

Frank and Joe left Rajiv's study and joined Vijay in the living room. Sachin had already gone to bed. Rajiv sent word with Ramlal that he would see Alok and Mahesh in the morning.

"If he were paying for this," Mahesh said, "I bet he wouldn't keep us waiting."

"Take it easy, man," Alok said lazily. "You got a good meal and a movie out of it, didn't you?" He pointed to the big-screen TV in front of them.

Mahesh got up to leave. "I can't watch this anymore. See you tomorrow," he said, and stalked out.

Alok shrugged, reluctantly pushed himself up from the couch, and followed.

Leaving Vijay sacked out in front of the TV, the Hardys headed upstairs for bed.

Minutes later Frank was ready to turn out the lights as Joe pulled his sheets back and started to get into bed. Joe suddenly froze.

"Leave the lights on," he said, keeping his voice low and steady.

Frank glanced over to see a cobra as thick as his forearm uncoil from the middle of Joe's bed and lift its head. Its neck flared out flat, and the snake let out an angry, catlike hiss.

"Don't move, Joe," Frank said. The head swayed in midair, inches from Joe's face.

Frank reached out slowly for the bronze Vishnu statue. He had it in his hand when the cobra hissed again, rose, and lunged at Joe, sinking its fangs deep into his shoulder.

Chapter

5

JOE STAGGERED BACK, grasping the writhing snake by its head. The cobra refused to let go, and Joe could only think of how it must be pumping venom into his shoulder. Finally he ripped the snake free and flung it to the floor.

Before the beady-eyed creature could slither under the bed, Frank slammed the sculpture down on its head, crushing it flat. The sound was like someone squashing a huge grasshopper on a sidewalk.

"Quick, someone call a doctor!" Frank yelled down the hall, then returned to his brother, who had slumped under the window, his face pale and slick with sweat.

Joe clutched his shoulder. One of the fangs had broken off and was still stuck in there; he could feel it with his fingers. Blood speckled his T-shirt, but his shoulder didn't hurt as much as he expected. The pain seemed dull and far away.

"Hang in there, Joe," Frank said.

Within seconds, Vijay, Sachin, and Rajiv appeared. "A cobra!" Rajiv exclaimed. "Sachin, call the doctor immediately."

"Stay still," Frank said to Joe. "You want to keep the poison from spreading too quickly." Joe just nodded his head.

"We haven't had snakes in a long time," Rajiv said, pulling the top sheet off Joe's bed and draping it around him.

"You mean they get into people's houses in the city?" Frank said.

"In some parts," Rajiv said. "It is unusual, though. Generally, they're in the street, and if someone in the neighborhood spots one, the snake has no chance. Everyone surrounds it and beats it to death. Sachin's younger brother died from a snakebite, I believe."

"That's nice to know," Joe said.

Sachin arrived with the doctor but refused to enter the room. He hovered at the doorway, unable to look at either Joe or the snake.

It was Dr. Das, the same one who had examined Frank earlier in the day, and he maintained his matter-of-fact attitude. He prodded the snake with his shoe, then lifted its head and opened its mouth. He pinched the snake's head, as if searching for something, then his round face broke into a grin.

"You are very, very lucky," he said to Joe. "This cobra's glands have been removed."

"What?" Joe asked, wondering when—or if—the doctor would produce some kind of antidote.

"There's no venom in this snake. It isn't from the wild. It probably belongs to a street performer and got loose. Pull off your shirt, please, and allow me to examine the wound."

The doctor took a quick look at Joe's shoulder, which had two neat puncture wounds. He produced a pair of tweezers from his black bag and, after a little prying, pulled the fang free. He then swabbed and dressed the puncture wounds. "You're going to be all right," he said.

Rajiv called one of his house servants to remove the dead snake. After that, Sachin stood by the window, peering out. "I guess it could have climbed up the trellis," he said doubtfully.

"Don't be ridiculous," Vijay scoffed. "It probably came up through a pipe or vent. Snakes don't climb walls."

"Enough," Rajiv said. "Let Frank and Joe sleep now. They could use the rest after everything they've been through today."

"Sachin," Vijay said. "As long as you're awake, you might as well give me a ride home."

"But it's midnight. Can't you take a cab?"

"Too much bother. Come on now," Vijay said. "It'll only take you twenty minutes or so at this hour." Sachin finally agreed, and their voices trailed off as they headed back downstairs. Minutes later Frank heard the car pull out of the driveway.

"This was not an accident," he said to Rajiv. "Snake charmers depend on cobras for a living. How often do they allow one to escape?"

"I'm inclined to agree with you," Rajiv said, stepping out into the hall. He looked first at Joe, then at Frank. "Why don't we all sleep on it and try to sort it out in the morning? Good night."

Frank was far from satisfied. He made Joe get in bed, then searched the room for vents. "The only way a snake could get in here is through the door or window," he said, raising his head from the floor where he was shining his penlight under the dresser. "Do you remember if you closed the door behind you when we went down to dinner?"

"I'm pretty sure I did," Joe said, making himself comfortable.

Frank checked the sock in Joe's bag; the beard was still there. He didn't think anyone had rifled their stuff.

Returning to the window, Frank searched the outer sill carefully with his flashlight. He spotted something the size and shape of a postage stamp in a corner near the edge. He picked it up and held it under the light. A thin, flexible piece of wood, rough on two ends, smooth on the other two. "Joe," he said. "This could be another clue."

But Joe didn't answer because he was already fast asleep.

On the set early the next morning Frank was assigned to help the second assistant load the film and keep track of the magazines. He had to write the details of each shot on the outside of the film canisters so the film editor could blend the hundreds of individual shots and scenes into one two-hour film.

Frank was anxious to do a little snooping around the set, but he and Joe had to be careful; they had to at least appear to be film students. The Hardys had decided to search the actors' dressing rooms, and Frank also figured that whoever had the chance should check out Mahesh's office. Of all the crew members, Mahesh seemed to be the most angry with Rajiv.

Joe, meanwhile, got to work moving props and furniture in the Hall of Public Audiences according to the production designer's plan. He was a short, squat man who spoke Hinglish—a mixture of Hindi and English—yet was able to make himself understood.

"Move that, *udhar,* I mean, over there," he said, pointing Joe to a corner of the room. *"Theek,* okay. Now go find the basket."

Joe took off down the hall; this was a chance to do some real sleuthing. He found Alok at his desk behind the screen, sketching an escape scene in which Vijay, or his double, would scale the palace wall. Joe told Alok what he'd come for.

"You mean the snake basket?" Alok asked.

"There isn't a snake in it, is there?" Joe asked, not wanting a repeat encounter with a reptile.

Alok shook his head. "Sachin says he couldn't find one. They're going to use a fake instead. He was relieved about that."

Mahesh emerged from his room shuffling through papers. "As if a live snake were even necessary," he groused.

Joe remembered the terror on Sachin's face the night before and Rajiv's remark about his younger brother dying of a snakebite.

"Too bad you guys didn't stick around last night," Joe joked. "I had a snake you could have used." Pulling down the collar of his shirt and revealing the bandage, he told Alok and Mahesh what had happened to him after they left.

"That was some joke," Alok said, frowning. His lips had gotten thin with anger. "I'd kill the person who did something like that to me."

"You are lucky to be alive, boy," Mahesh said. He was amazed. "Even Sachin wouldn't go that far."

"What do you mean?" Joe asked.

"He's a prankster. He put live salamanders in Kamala's jewelry box once and a whoopee cushion under Tariq's seat on the dais."

"Childish stuff," Alok said. "But basically

harmless. Vijay was so mad he threatened to have Sachin fired.''

"He thinks because he's the producer's nephew, he has control on the set," Mahesh said. "Rajiv and Sachin have been working together for five years. Sachin's the son Rajiv never had, and he would never take Vijay's side over him."

Back on the set, Kamala and Tariq were ready to shoot but Vijay was late—again. Frank watched Tariq pace back and forth, his slippers slapping against the mottled green marble floor.

"He's getting into character," Kamala whispered mischievously. "Not that it's much of a stretch."

"What do you mean?"

"Only that he's a pompous old fool, which is exactly what the guru is."

Remembering Joe's encounter with Tariq the day before, Frank asked, "Did Tariq know Ram Jagannath?"

"He'd never heard of Jagannath until the audition," Kamala said.

"How about you? Did you ever see the guru in real life?"

Kamala shook her head.

"So, what interested you most about this film?" Frank asked.

Kamala sighed. "As I told your brother, I wanted the opportunity to work with Rajiv. This was supposed to be my break-out role."

"And now you just want out?"

"I can't get out of my contract now. Believe me, if I could afford to, I would."

Rajiv interrupted her from across the room.

"Kamala, why don't you and Tariq run through the scene with Nikhil? He knows all the lines."

Just then Joe returned with the snake basket. He put it in its place at the foot of Ram Jagannath's ornately carved chair and came over to Frank.

"I hope they've got a lively one in there," Frank joked.

"It's fake. Believe me, I checked," Joe said. "I've got to go back and help Mahesh."

"Hey," Frank said in a whisper. "I forgot to tell you I found something last night, but if you've got to go, I'll talk to you later."

"Great," Joe said as he turned and disappeared down the hallway.

Kamala, Nikhil, and Tariq began their scene. Frank could see that Kamala wasn't as enthusiastic as her costars. She barely looked at Nikhil. In response, he said his lines with extra energy as if trying to compensate for Kamala's underacting.

"Kamala," Rajiv said, interrupting them midscene, "you're going to have to work up a little more emotion. Your guru has just told you that you can't marry the man that you love."

"I'm trying," Kamala said. "Anyway, we're just rehearsing here. You'll have some real tears from me when the star gets here." She stressed the word *star* with a little toss of her head.

Minutes later Vijay appeared. Nikhil gave up his place, and Rajiv had Tariq, Kamala, and Vijay run through the scene again. Unfortunately, Vijay's presence didn't seem to help Kamala drum up any emotion. If anything, she was having a harder time crying on cue.

"My dear, it looks like we're going to have to use the glycerin," Rajiv said. "And you know how fake those tears look."

"Oh, go ahead, use the glycerin," Kamala said. "It doesn't matter to me."

Rajiv asked Frank to fetch the glycerin from the makeup room. The truth was, Frank thought as he made his way down the hall, Kamala was a pretty awful actress. He grabbed one of several bottles of clear glycerin from a small table by the door. He hurried back to the set and handed the bottle to Kamala.

"Good thing Biku isn't here to see this," Nikhil whispered under his breath to Frank.

"What do you mean?" Frank asked.

"She's angry because they were engaged when she first signed for the film. Then he fled to London and dumped her, but she's still stuck with her contract. I heard she lost other offers because of this."

Rajiv called for silence on the set as the actors prepared. The hum of activity quickly quieted to dead silence. A makeup artist took a final swipe at Kamala's hair with a brush, then darted out of the picture. Microphones hung from the high, frescoed ceiling, and cameras were stationed on booms and tracks all around the actors. This would be the master shot, the one that included everyone, the one that would be shot from many angles and perspectives.

"Okay," Rajiv said. "Let's—"

He was interrupted by a shriek from Kamala. "My eyes, my eyes! I can't see!"

Chapter

6

FRANK RAN TO KAMALA, who stood in front of
the cameras, her hands over her eyes. "Hold everything," Rajiv yelled as Kamala's shrieks sub-
sided into sobbing.

"Don't rub your eyes," Frank said, leading her
to a chair. "It's only going to make it worse."
Nikhil stood next to him, nodding in agreement
as he awkwardly patted Kamala on the shoulder
to comfort her.

Rajiv ordered Sachin to call the doctor. Spying
Mahesh in the corner, Rajiv strode over to him,
deliberately slapping his clipboard against his
right thigh with each step.

"You!" He pointed to Mahesh and launched
into a tirade in Hindi, occasionally punctuated
with English phrases to emphasize his points.

"Mahesh already has enough trouble," Nikhil whispered to Frank.

"What did he do?"

"Right now Rajiv is blaming him for the glycerin. But last week Rajiv found out that Mahesh was moonlighting on another production, so Rajiv is withholding his pay until the end of the shoot."

"Who told on Mahesh?"

Vijay, who was standing behind them, shrugged. "Rajiv received an anonymous call, and when he confronted Mahesh, Mahesh said it was true. They had a huge fight, and Mahesh accused him of cheating the crew."

"What do you mean?" Frank asked. "He can't make people work against their wills."

"No, but you heard Mahesh last night at dinner. There are no unions, and according to the terms of their contracts, all crew members must stay on the set as long as Rajiv requires them."

Before Frank could ask any other questions, Rajiv called him over to a corner.

"You're supposed to watch out for things like this," he hissed, waving the glycerin bottle in front of Frank's nose. "Where did you find this bottle?"

"In the makeup room," Frank said quietly. He didn't want anyone overhearing their conversation. "Everyone has access to it. We can't monitor all these people." Frank took the bottle from

Rajiv. "And now there's no way to check for fingerprints since you've all been handling this."

"That may be," Rajiv whispered, "but I want results, and I want them soon. You boys came highly recommended, so don't disappoint me."

Frank sighed. He hoped Joe was having better luck.

After finding the basket, Joe had returned to the prop room, near where Alok was working on the escape scene. He held a gleaming, three-pronged grappling hook in his hand and was tying a rope to it.

"Mahesh says you are to pick out some books to go in Ram Jagannath's library," Alok said.

"Sure." Joe went to the long prop shelves and started stacking together old books that looked as if they might contain spiritual wisdom. Joe wondered if Alok was as disgruntled as Mahesh had been at dinner. "What do you think about Rajiv's treatment of the crew?" he asked.

"Many people are upset," Alok said. He let a foot or two of the rope slide through his hands and swung the heavy steel hook in the air, as if testing its balance. "All I know is that I have nothing to complain about."

"The way you handle some of your props, that's good to hear," Joe said, gesturing toward the grapnel as it was whipped through the air.

Alok smiled and let the hook dangle at his feet. "I was out of the business for a long time," he said. "When I came back, I had lost all my contacts. Rajiv Kapoor was the only director who would hire me, so I'm lucky to have this job." He turned to leave. "I'm going outside to test this on a wall. Keep sorting those books."

Once he was alone, Joe abandoned the books. He walked around the next divider to the counter lined with Styrofoam heads. It was just as Frank had described. There were twelve or fifteen heads, each with a different style and color of wig on it. Some of them also had matching beards and mustaches, but it wasn't obvious that one set was missing. Joe found a blue binder on the end of the counter containing a log of all the clothes and accessories. The number of sets of wigs and facial hair matched the number the log said should be there.

Joe wasn't convinced. It wouldn't be hard to alter the entries in the book. He went down the line, holding each hairpiece up to the light to check its color exactly. Toward the end of the line, he picked up one wig that seemed heavier than the ones before it. The hair was especially thick, and the color seemed to match the beard Frank had ripped from the fake Sachin's face. There was only one way to be sure; Joe had to make a direct comparison.

But the toupee was too big to tuck under his shirt or in the pocket of his jeans; he had to figure out another way to get it out of there.

Joe went behind the screen to Alok's desk and

opened each drawer. Nothing. He stopped for a second, listening for any sound of Mahesh returning or the guard making his rounds. All was quiet. He glanced up at the balcony above. He could only hope no one was spying on him through the stone slats.

Quickly he entered Mahesh's office to look for scissors. He didn't find any, but did discover something almost as good. There, in the very back of the top drawer of Mahesh's desk, Joe found a gold-handled dagger with a razor-sharp four-inch blade. The handle was encrusted with emeralds and rubies, and the weight of it surprised Joe.

Careful to choose a place where the damage wouldn't be too obvious, Joe cut a lock of hair from the toupee and then put both the dagger and the hairpiece back where he'd found them.

Tucking the loose hair in his pocket, Joe then went over to the costume racks. He ran his fingers along the hangers, looking for the red tunic the fake Sachin had worn. He didn't see it. He squeezed his way between two racks of silk scarves and embroidered tunics. On the floor he found a foot locker piled to the brim with at least fifty preassembled red turbans. They were exactly like the one the fake Sachin had been wearing. Joe checked the inventory book. According to the records, one turban had been assigned to Tariq, a second to Nikhil, and a third to Vijay.

* * *

Meanwhile, Dr. Das had arrived to check Kamala's eyes. He glanced around the set and said, "What, no snakebite this time?"

Kamala was no longer crying. She sat calmly with her eyes hidden behind sunglasses. The doctor examined her briefly, holding her eyelids back carefully and shining his light in her eyes as he had her roll her pupils around. Then he took a look at her cheeks, which were streaked with tears.

"Well," he said as he stood up. "She's okay. There are traces of finely ground red pepper on her face. I believe it was in the glycerin. There will be burning and stinging for some time but I will prescribe an ophthalmic rinse, and she will be fine."

He packed up his bag as he spoke and said to Kamala, "Of course, you'll call me if you have any other problems."

"Doctor," she said, with a slight smile, "I will have problems as long as I work here, but not the kind you can help me with."

Frank asked the doctor how he thought the glycerin had gotten contaminated.

"It's hard to say," the doctor said. "But you need only a small amount of cayenne to affect the eyes. It could have been on someone's hands, or else someone could have been eating in the room on the table near the glycerin and sprinkled pepper a little sloppily."

"Those sound like long shots to me," Frank said.

"Perhaps," the doctor said, peering over the top of his glasses. "It depends on whether you're looking for an accident or a deliberate action."

After he left, they went back to shooting the scene. Kamala seemed ready and willing to work. In fact, with her eyes still stinging, she was able to shed plenty of real tears. Rajiv was practically giggling, and he congratulated Kamala several times as he tried the shot from every possible angle. Then his mood changed quickly.

"Cut!" he yelled in the middle of the seventh shot. "What is that noise outside?" A loud shout followed by arguing and heavy footsteps penetrated the double doors. "We can't possibly work with these constant interruptions. Sachin, Frank, tell the caterers or whoever is out there to be quiet. Please get rid of them."

Sachin and Frank hurried over to the heavy wooden doors and opened them, prepared to shoo away whoever was there. Instead, Frank came face-to-face with two police officers in uniform, accompanied by a tall man in a charcoal-colored suit. The guard stood behind them, looking apologetic.

"I tried to tell them to wait, but they wouldn't listen," he said.

"What's the problem, sir?" Frank asked.

"I'm Detective Lieutenant Bedi," the man in the suit said, flipping open his wallet and flashing his badge. He was a couple of inches taller than Frank but very thin. "We're looking for Vijay Tate." Bedi pushed past Frank and Sachin and strode up to Rajiv.

"I assume you're Rajiv Kapoor," the detective said. "Where is Tate?"

"Right here, Officer," Vijay said, stepping forward. "What seems to be the problem? Did anther fan break into my apartment?"

"No," Bedi said, seizing Vijay by the elbow, "you're under arrest. Come with us."

Chapter

7

"WHAT?" VIJAY LOOKED SHOCKED. "What are you talking about?"

"Your suitcase was found at the airport containing several kilos of Semtex plastic explosive," Detective Bedi said. "We're taking you down to police headquarters to question you. Let's go."

Kamala gasped; Nikhil and Rajiv stepped in.

"You can't just take him down there like that," Rajiv said, reaching for Detective Bedi's arm. "We're in the middle of a costly filming schedule. He's our leading man. We have attorneys who can address this problem."

Bedi shoved Rajiv's hand away and nodded to a uniformed officer, who locked a pair of handcuffs around Vijay's wrists.

"We certainly can take him away," the detective

said. "Under current law, anyone suspected of terrorism must be taken into custody and questioned immediately. In matters of national security we can't be concerned with filming schedules."

Vijay was shaking his head. "I don't understand. What do you mean about my suitcase? I have nothing to do with smuggling explosives. Rajiv, we must be able to settle this some other way."

"Can you be more specific about the charges, Lieutenant?" Frank asked.

"Stay out of this," Bedi snapped at Frank. "Let's go," he said, taking Vijay by the arm and leading him out the door. "Any more trouble and I'll charge you with resisting arrest."

"Sachin!" Rajiv thundered, marching down the hall. "Get the lawyers on the phone. We must get Vijay out of jail immediately."

"What suitcase are they talking about?" Mahesh asked. "Vijay flew in the day before yesterday."

"The airline left one of his bags behind in London," Frank said. "They sent it on the flight yesterday, and Sachin was supposed to pick it up, but he couldn't get through all the traffic."

Kamala stood with her hands on her hips. "This is ridiculous," she said. Her makeup was running where the tears had rolled down her cheeks. "What are we going to do now?"

Alok came running in from outside, the grappling hook in his hand and a coil of rope over his shoulder. "I just saw the police leave with Vijay," he said. "What's going on?"

Frank filled him in.

"There must be some kind of mistake," Alok said. "Why would Vijay jeopardize his career with smuggling?"

"Don't worry," Mahesh said, his voice dripping with sarcasm. "I'm sure our fearless leader will have it all sorted out by tomorrow."

"Without Vijay, there's no film," Kamala said. "Rajiv wouldn't let his beloved star rot in prison, would he?"

Her question hung in the air as many among the cast and crew exchanged glances. Unless Rajiv could bail Vijay out quickly, this might be the incident that finished the film, Frank thought. Biku had backed the production with a guaranteed role for his nephew. With Vijay gone, Biku might back out, taking all his money and investors with him. Then the cast and crew would be free to sign on with other directors, leaving Rajiv in the dust.

Unaware of the interruption on the set, Joe had sneaked from the prop room to the actors' dressing rooms, which were located on the other side of a well-lit, plant-filled atrium, in what used to be the women's quarters. Their doors were all shut, and Kamala's was still the only one with any sort of identification—the gold star on the doorknob.

Joe picked a door at random and went in. This room was more spare than Kamala's, with a cracked marble floor and whitewashed stone walls. Clothes hung neatly inside a metal wardrobe in the corner. Joe reached up to the top shelf and felt around, pulling out a pair of men's dress shoes and then one of the red turbans.

He quickly checked the drawers of the dressing table in front of the mirror. Something in the top drawer snagged as he tried to close it. Pulling the drawer completely out, Joe discovered a creased color photograph of a woman with short, dark brown hair wearing old-fashioned, cat-eye sunglasses. She held a boy of three or four years old, who looked a lot like Nikhil. The sunlight was bright, and the photo had been overexposed. Standing behind the woman and child was a tall man with blond hair, who squinted at the camera and didn't smile.

As he tried to get the drawer to slide back onto its track, Joe heard footsteps. As they became louder, Joe shut the drawer, clicked off the light, and scrambled into the wardrobe. Hearing someone grasp the door handle, Joe managed to pull one door shut, but the other was warped and wouldn't stay closed. He hooked the edge with his finger and held it, hoping that whoever came in wouldn't notice.

Someone entered the room, walked over to the dressing table, and turned on the lamp there.

Peering through the crack between the doors,

Joe saw it was Nikhil. He pulled out a cellular phone, punched in some numbers, and then turned his back to Joe.

"It's me. No, no, don't worry. No bad news."

Why wasn't Nikhil on the set? Joe wondered. He heard Nikhil pause, then continue, speaking very softly.

"Don't worry. We've been given the afternoon off. The police came and arrested Vijay." He paused again. "No, no, they have no idea. Anyway, it may not matter if the film gets canceled." Another pause. "Yes, three days. I'll meet you at seven A.M. at the Taj Mahal Hotel. Yes, goodbye."

Nikhil left the room and hurried off down the hall.

Joe slipped out of the wardrobe and stood in front of the dressing table. What had Vijay done to get himself arrested? Joe looked in the mirror and tried to imagine Nikhil with sunglasses, a red turban, and heavy facial hair. Nikhil was the right height to be the man who'd picked them up at the airport, but why would he want to sabotage the film? Had he set up Vijay so he could take his place in the movie?

Joe studied the photograph, committing as many of its details as possible to memory. It was now clear that the child in the picture was Nikhil, and the woman and man must be his parents.

Figuring he'd waited long enough for Nikhil to be far away, Joe put the photo back in the drawer and headed back to the set. When he got to the Hall of Public Audiences, he found Frank labeling film cans. Rajiv and Sachin were deep in conversation, going over lists on a clipboard, while Mahesh and some of the technicians rolled up cables and put away lights. The actors were nowhere in sight.

"What's going on?" Joe asked.

"Someone laced Kamala's glycerin with hot pepper," Frank said. "Then the cops came and took Vijay in for questioning." Frank lowered his voice. "I think Vijay's bag may have been the reason for all the chaos at the airport. The police think he's smuggling plastic explosives into the country."

"Sounds like I missed a couple of major developments," Joe said. "I've got some news, too."

"Excellent," Frank said. "What is it?"

Joe was going to answer, but he saw Sachin approaching and had to clam up.

"We're done for the day," Sachin said. "We'll go back to Rajiv's and wait for news about Vijay."

"It must be killing Rajiv to let us out early tonight," Mahesh said as he and the Hardys left the palace. "After all, it's only seven-thirty."

"Do you have plans?" Frank asked, wondering if Mahesh was still trying to moonlight for that other director.

"My cousin and her family are in town," he replied. "We are all going out for dinner."

With a wave, he walked away, leaving the Hardys to wait for Sachin and the car.

"He was in a good mood for once," Joe said.

"I noticed," Frank said. "He's the one person who didn't seem too worried about Vijay being carted off."

Across the street the textile factory was dark, closed for the night. Lights flickered in the makeshift huts that crowded around it. As they got into the car, Frank asked Sachin where the electricity for the huts came from.

"The workers bribe the local inspector and tap into the main power lines," Sachin said. "It goes on everywhere. Bribery is a way of life these days."

He must be exaggerating, Frank thought, but he dropped the subject. Rajiv had hurried over to the car and was waiting for them. And he didn't look as if he was in the mood for a discussion about local corruption.

Back at Rajiv's place they ate dinner mostly in silence. A telephone call interrupted the main course, and Rajiv took it in his office.

"Vijay is going before a judge tomorrow morning to be formally charged with smuggling and terrorism," he said when he came back. "The lawyers think they can get him released on bail, but the evidence is overwhelming." Rajiv rubbed his eyes in exhaustion. "The bag looks exactly like his; it has all his clothes and papers in it.

More importantly, the tag matches the one on his ticket."

Rajiv motioned to Sachin. "Leave us for a moment, please."

Once Sachin had padded upstairs, Rajiv produced two envelopes for the Hardys. "Here," he said. "I got you two and Sachin invitations to Alex Chandraswamy's party tomorrow night. See what you can find out. We must clear Vijay's name."

Frank and Joe took the envelopes, promising a break in the case soon, and headed to their room. When they got there, Joe closed the door quickly and plunged his hand into his pocket.

"Take a look at this, Frank," he said, placing the tuft of dark hair on top of the nightstand. "I cut it off one of the toupees in the prop room."

Frank retrieved the beard from Joe's sock and compared it to the hairs on the table. The color was the same, as was the texture. "I'd say we have a pretty good match," he said. "Nice going."

"That's not all," Joe said. "I found a trunk full of red turbans just like the one the fake Sachin was wearing at the airport. Nikhil, Vijay, and Alok—they all have one as part of their costumes."

"That doesn't mean one of those guys was the fake Sachin," Frank said. "Anyone on the set could have sneaked in and taken a turban from that trunk."

"True," Joe said, pointing at Frank. "But what about this? I was searching Nikhil's room and he came in to make a phone call. I was hiding in the closet. I heard everything he said." Joe recounted Nikhil's end of the conversation.

"It sounds to me like he might have set Vijay up for arrest," Frank said. "But why would he want Vijay in jail? Sure, he steps into the lead role, but there's no guarantee that the movie can even go on without Vijay."

They were both stumped.

"The last thing Nikhil said to whoever he called was that he'd meet them at the Taj Mahal Hotel in three days at seven in the morning," Joe said. "It sounded important."

"Three days," Frank said. "That's Friday. Let's make a point of joining Nikhil and his friend for breakfast. I wouldn't be surprised if it's someone outside the production with a very serious interest in seeing Rajiv go down in flames."

Frank remembered that he hadn't told Joe about the distinctive wood chip he'd found on the windowsill the night before. He was about to say something about it when the lights in the room flickered and went out.

Frank and Joe ran into the hall, where they found Sachin standing in the moonlight in front of the glass double doors leading out to the balcony. He was shaking a flashlight, but it wouldn't come on.

"What's up?" Joe asked.

"Power failure," Sachin said. "It happens all the time. The system is antiquated."

Joe looked out the glass doors just in time to see a dark object come arcing over the balcony railing right toward his head.

"Incoming," Joe yelled, and they all hit the deck.

One of the big glass doors shattered, showering shards of glass all over. A black marble globe the size of a softball thumped down and rolled to the end of the hallway.

Jumping up, Frank saw someone dressed in black run down the driveway. He eased himself out the doors, carefully avoiding the jagged edges, and climbed over the railing, dropping to the cement below. He took off up the street and spotted the vandal darting between two parked cars and then up a grassy hill into the darkness.

Frank slowed to a jog. He went past the spot where the figure had disappeared and found a brick drive leading into a wooded park. He walked up the drive. On either side of him trees and dense shrubs rustled in the breeze, casting dark shadows in the moonlight. Frank knew his chances of finding anyone were slim—there were too many places to hide. For all he knew, the guy was already on the other side of the park, jogging down the road and congratulating himself on his easy escape.

Back at the entrance to the park, Frank paused

and looked around to make sure he hadn't missed anything.

As he turned, a powerful arm snaked under his chin, jerking his head back and exposing his neck. Then he felt a cold, sharp blade against his jugular vein.

"Move and I'll slit your throat."

Chapter

8

FRANK FELT THE KNIFE pressing into his neck and the breath caught in his throat.

"Give Rajiv a message for us," a voice hissed in Frank's ear. "If he doesn't quit, we're going to—"

At that instant a car screeched around the corner and sped up the park drive, headlights bobbing in the darkness.

Frank grabbed the man's knife hand, dropped, and twisted. He had almost executed a perfect reversal—ending up behind his attacker with the man locked in an arm hold—when the assailant dropped the knife and slipped free, disappearing into the trees.

Frank started to follow, but a hand grabbed him by the elbow. It was Joe. "You okay, Frank?"

"I think so. Let's go after him."

"What's the point?" Joe said. "So you can get ambushed again?"

"I guess you're right," Frank said. "We could slink around this park all night and still not find him."

Frank moved into the glare of the headlights and probed his neck for damage. His fingers came away clean.

"You've got a nice red mark," Joe said, leaning in. "One good slice in that spot and you were a goner."

"The guy knew what he was doing," Frank said. "He was quick and quiet—and strong. He said something about giving Rajiv a message from 'us.' He never finished the threat. Anyway, it sounds like there's more than one person involved."

"Unless it's Tariq," Joe said with a chuckle. "He has a tendency to use the royal we."

Frank smiled. "Tariq? If he's that good, then let's recruit him to work for us." Frank started searching the ground around them. "He dropped the knife here somewhere, but we won't get any prints. Just about the only thing I did notice was that the guy was wearing gloves. There it is." Frank bent down and picked up a dagger. It had a gold handle encrusted with jewels that sparkled in the headlights.

"That's Mahesh's knife," Joe said. "I found it in his desk this morning."

"I doubt it belongs to Mahesh," Frank said. "Look, it has the maharaja's family crest at the bottom. This knife belongs at the palace, all right, but not in the production manager's desk."

Frank and Joe got in the car to drive back to the house. "How'd you get the car to come after me?" Frank asked.

"Sachin gave me the keys." Joe said. "He was in such a panic, I didn't think he'd be able to find them. He kept bumping around in the dark like a mole in a maze."

"Well, you got to the park just in time." Frank tucked the dagger into his sleeve, where no one would see it. He needed time to think, and he didn't want Rajiv and Sachin to go into another panic.

They pulled up at the house and found Sachin standing just inside the open front door, wearing a red bathrobe. "Did you catch him?" Sachin asked.

"Nope, he got away," said Joe.

"Perhaps we should call the police."

"No way. Any kind of investigation would definitely shut down the production," Frank said. "Maybe Joe and I will see what we can figure out."

Upstairs Rajiv stood over Ramlal, who busily swept up the broken glass.

Rajiv handed Frank the black marble globe that had come crashing through the window. "It's from the palace," he said. "My family will be very upset to find I'm watching over their things so carelessly."

"Don't worry," Sachin said to his boss. "We'll find the saboteur and put an end to this."

Rajiv looked at his assistant and sighed. "Just stick to what you're good at, Sachin," the filmmaker said. "We'll sort this out without any extra interference."

Since no one knew when Vijay would be released, Rajiv had decided they would film the exteriors on an estate north of the city the next day. It was a two-hour drive, so they would be waking up even earlier than usual. The Hardys said their good nights and went back to their room where Frank laid all their physical evidence out on his bed—the globe, the knife, the beard, and the chip of wood. First, he told Joe where he found the chip, then he said, "What do you think?"

Joe stretched his arms over his head with a big groan. "One thing's obvious. Everything except this piece of wood came from the production set."

"And everyone in the cast and crew had access to all of this stuff except the knife," Frank noted. "The guy who attacked me could've been Mahesh. He seemed about the same height, but something just doesn't feel right."

"I still think Nikhil is involved, too," Joe said,

picking up the chip of wood and turning it over in his palm. "And I think I know what this is."

"What?" Frank moved in closer.

"It looks like a piece of the snake basket on the set," Joe said. "I got a good look at it. It was made of long strips of wood woven together, and it was kind of beaten up."

"So we can assume someone brought in the cobra in a basket," Frank said. He went to open the windows and looked down. It was easily eighteen feet to the ground. "The guy I chased tonight could have climbed up the trellis."

"With the basket under his arm?"

"Or strapped to his back." Frank turned back to the center of the room.

"Hey, close the window," Joe said. "I don't feel like letting in any more cobras." He scooped the evidence off Frank's bed and carried it to the dresser.

"Hold on," Frank said, taking the dagger from Joe. "I want to show this to Mahesh tomorrow and see his reaction."

As they lay in their beds in the dark, Joe spoke up.

"I was just thinking, Frank," he said. "If someone was trying to frame Vijay for smuggling explosives, they would have had to have access to his luggage at the airport."

"That's right," Frank said. "And if bribery is as rampant here as Sachin said, how hard would it be for Mahesh or anyone else to infiltrate security at the airport and pay somebody to plant Semtex in Vijay's suitcase?"

"Not very hard at all," Joe said.

They left for the maharaja's country estate before sunrise. The car was quiet for most of the drive, with Rajiv planning the day's shoot and Sachin driving at speeds that would be illegal on any road back in Bayport. Frank read through the script, looking forward to seeing some exotic animals—definitely elephants, and possibly tigers, though he'd heard that tigers were a protected species kept on government reserves.

Meanwhile, Joe leafed through the various articles in one of Rajiv's files. The character of Ram Jagannath was difficult to pin down. He was an Englishman who'd passed as an Indian and amassed a tremendous following. While he preached love and peace, he was involved in smuggling arms and explosives and selling them to the highest bidder, with no allegiance to one group or another. Could there be any connection between Jagannath's smuggling and Vijay Tate's case?

Joe was struck by the fact that there were no photographs of the guru. It did make sense, however, given the identity he wanted to maintain.

The estate took up over twenty square miles of land and was bisected by the River Tansa. According to the script, the shoot would take place in a clearing by the river. When the Hardys arrived, they found several members of the crew strapping a series of belts and harnesses around a camera operator who was built like a linebacker.

"What are you doing there?" Joe asked.

"We're rigging up this Steadicam," the cameraman said. He held up a 16mm camera attached to a Z-shaped arm with spring-loaded joints. "Once I hook this arm onto these belts, I can follow the action anywhere, and the camera won't shake at all. The picture will be as smooth as if the camera were stuck to a tripod on the ground."

Joe wanted to stay and watch the Steadicam in action, but Sachin called him and Frank over to help unload lights, cables, and film cans from an old, beaten-up delivery van. Frank lugged an eight-foot-tall light stand to the edge of the clearing, then watched four other crew members push a reflector the size of a kettledrum to the bank of the river. It left behind a wide track of flattened grass. As he walked back to the van, Frank glanced into the thick woods around them. If any wild animals were around, they were keeping quiet. He did see Mahesh over by the caterer's table, alternately sipping a cup of coffee and paging through some notes. Like Frank and Joe, the rest of the crew was busy unloading and setting up.

At the table Frank poured himself some juice. He wanted to start a casual conversation, then surprise Mahesh with the knife. "I'm kind of disappointed not to see any animals," he said. "Especially after coming all this way."

Mahesh looked up. "No, and I don't see the gameskeeper, either. He was supposed to meet me here." Mahesh rolled his eyes. "All he cares about is that we don't destroy any property or kill any animals—although I doubt any of them would come near this noisy bunch."

Frank was about to pull out the knife and show it to Mahesh when a big black sedan roared into the clearing and came to a stop next to the makeup trailer in a cloud of dust. Kamala, Tariq, and Nikhil all got out and walked toward Frank and Mahesh. Kamala's dresser, Minni, went to the car's trunk, pulled out an armful of costumes, and stepped into the trailer. Nikhil handed Kamala a cup of tea. Turning to Mahesh, he said, "How was your dinner last night?"

Frank watched Tariq stuff an entire buttered muffin in his mouth.

"It was fun," Mahesh replied. "We went to the Copper Chimney to eat, and then I took my cousin dancing."

"Where's she from?"

"The States," Mahesh said. "New York City, actually. Didn't you say you were from close to there?"

"Uh, yes," Frank said, surprised.

Mahesh grinned. "Well, maybe you will get a chance to meet her, though not on this set, since relatives are forbidden." Mahesh nodded toward

Rajiv, who was gesturing for Joe to move some lights a little closer. "Not that there's going to be a set for much longer."

"Rajiv seems to think Vijay will get out on bail," Frank said.

Nikhil chimed in. "If he has a lenient judge, that is. Many officials actually become very annoyed when movie stars flout the law."

"You act as if you think he's guilty," Frank said.

"Oh, no," Mahesh answered. "Nikhil doesn't think Vijay's a smuggler; he knows Vijay doesn't have the brains for that sort of thing. He's only saying that Vijay doesn't believe any of society's rules apply to him."

Kamala interrupted them. "Enough of this talk," she said, tossing her hair. "I'm going to get dressed."

Kamala was halfway to her trailer when a crashing sound came from the woods. Joe looked up and saw a wild boar charge into the clearing, snorting furiously and darting its bloodshot little eyes around as it headed straight for the actress.

Chapter

9

THE BOAR STOPPED less than ten feet from Kamala, pawing the ground and swinging its huge shovel-shaped head from side to side. Kamala started to back up, then she screamed, and the boar charged, grunting and frothing at the mouth, its bristly hair standing on end.

As he rushed from his spot across the clearing, Joe glimpsed a metallic flash, then heard a high-pitched squeal. The boar fell to the ground, tumbling to a stop at Kamala's feet, where it twitched for a few seconds, stiffened, and went still.

When Joe reached Kamala, she collapsed in his arms. "Are you all right?" he asked.

She took a deep breath, paused dramatically, and said, "I could have been killed. Who's in charge of controlling these beasts?"

"The gamekeeper, if there is one," Joe mumbled, helping steady Kamala on her feet. He bent to examine the dead beast as the others crowded around. When he saw the jewel-encrusted gold handle of the dagger sticking out of the boar's thick neck, he looked up at his brother with a big grin and said, "Nice throw, Frank."

"Thanks, Joe," Frank said with a wink. "Just a lucky shot."

Moments later the gamekeeper, dressed in full safari outfit, finally showed up. He had the compact body of a gymnast and gestured wildly, waving his hands over his head when he saw the dead boar. "Who's responsible for this? We have laws about killing wildlife," he cried.

"If it hadn't been for our American friends, this animal could easily have killed Kamala while the rest of these fools stood around and gaped," Rajiv said. "You told me it would be safe to film here."

The gamekeeper started to reply, but Rajiv held up his hand, silencing him, and turned back to Frank. "By the way, where did you get this dagger? It belongs to the maharaja and should stay in the palace."

"Tell that to Mahesh," Joe said. "I saw it in his desk yesterday, and then whoever it was we chased last night after they broke your window almost slit Frank's throat with it."

"Is this true?" Rajiv raised his bushy eyebrows and turned to Mahesh.

79

Mahesh was startled. "I had no idea the dagger was in my desk," he said. "Someone must have planted it there." He seemed to be fumbling for excuses. "Or maybe they hoped the guard would find it in my possession. I don't know anything about that knife."

"Where were you at around eleven o'clock last night?" Frank asked.

"Out dancing with my cousin, as I said," Mahesh retorted, regaining his composure. "And I can prove it. There were many witnesses."

"You can bet someone will check up on that," Joe said.

"Mahesh," Rajiv said, his teeth clenched, "I would fire you right now except I know that's exactly what you want me to do. You'll see this project through to its finish. And you will not cause any more confusion."

After this exchange, everyone dispersed to give the gamekeeper room to back his truck in and remove the boar. It took four strong crew members, each grasping one leg, to load the carcass.

Kamala once again proved that even if she wasn't much of an actress, she did believe in the motto "The show must go on," and gamely went through her scenes for the rest of the day. Frank and Joe kept their eyes on Nikhil and Mahesh.

By sunset Rajiv was ready to call it a day. As they were leaving, he received a phone call. After he hung up, he made an announcement to the entire cast and crew.

"Good news, everyone," he said with a rare smile. "Vijay has been released on bail. We'll resume shooting tomorrow, as previously planned." He turned to Sachin and the Hardys. "Vijay is going to meet us at the house. Sachin can take you all to the party tonight."

"But we only have three passes," Sachin said.

Rajiv was conciliatory. "Look, Sachin, the poor fellow just spent the night in jail. Let him have your invitation. I'll make it up to you later, I promise."

Sachin looked disappointed but said nothing.

"Maybe we can sneak you in," Joe said as they got into the car.

Frank, however, was relieved that Sachin wouldn't be going. It might be a party, but they needed to get some work done, and Sachin, with his well-intentioned bumbling, would only be in the way.

Alex Chandraswamy's opening night ceremony and reception was being held at the Hotel Majestic, a five-star establishment on Juhu Beach. Vijay, Frank, and Joe left Sachin in the parking lot, where all the other drivers stayed, leaning against their cars. Sachin pulled out a book on screenwriting and said, "Might as well do some work while I wait."

As they walked under the long canvas awning to the entrance, Vijay said, "It's just as well

Sachin waits in the parking lot. He's only interested in gawking at the stars."

The hotel lobby was one of the most lavish Frank had ever seen. It was a huge space, lined on both sides with exclusive shops selling clothing and jewelry. A gauntlet of photographers extended the length of the lobby, leading to the ballroom way in the back. Frank and Joe found themselves flinching at the constant flashes as photographers jostled one another to get shots of Vijay, the rising star.

"Everyone will be here tonight," Vijay said, his eyes gleaming. "Tonight you'll see the social side of Bollywood. Many of these dramas are more interesting than anything you'll see on the screen."

Huge crystal chandeliers hung from the ceiling of the ballroom. The wallpaper had a gold background and was covered with red vines that twisted up and out of sight. The Hardys and Vijay made a circuit of the room, with the young actor stopping to shake hands all around.

At one end of the room there was a small stage draped in red velvet. "That's where the producers and director stand to make speeches," Vijay said. "And where the Hindu priest blesses the film."

"A blessing for the film?" Joe asked.

"Yes, usually you have a *pooja,* a prayer ceremony, at the beginning of a shoot, and then the *mahurat* when the actual film is released. This, of course, is the *mahurat,*" Vijay said, giving the Hardys a nod and leaving to talk to a tall man with black, slicked-back hair.

Frank and Joe moved along the rear of the ballroom. Enormous plate-glass windows overlooked the patio and pool area, which was lit by the soft glow of Chinese lanterns. Out beyond the patio small waves lapped at the beach.

"Hey, look," Joe said as he and Frank made their way to the buffet. "There's Mahesh. What's he doing here?"

Standing next to Mahesh at the buffet table was a pretty young woman with shoulder-length black hair and wearing a short red dress. She and Mahesh were both piling their plates with food.

"At last," Joe said as they approached them. "Someone with an appetite I can respect."

"Oh, hello, boys," Mahesh said. "This is my cousin Asha. She'll be glad to confirm where I was last night."

Asha looked confused. "Mahesh," she said. "Were you supposed to be somewhere else last night? I told you I could take care of myself."

"Not at all," Frank said. "Actually, we're glad Mahesh got out last night. He's had to put in too many hours on the set lately."

Mahesh seemed to relax. "Asha, please meet Frank and Joe Hardy. They are here from the States—Bayport to be precise."

"Bayport?" Asha said. "There's a great pizza parlor there called Mr. Pizza."

"You go to Mr. Pizza?" Joe said. "That's our favorite hangout."

"I can't believe we haven't run into each other there," Frank added.

"I'm away at college most of the time," Asha said, adding a hot *samosa* to her plate. Joe recognized the tasty pastries that were stuffed with potato filling from their first meal at Rajiv's.

"So, did you get an invitation in the mail?" Joe asked casually as they made their way along the buffet table, taking large portions of each dish.

"Mahesh knows the producer of this movie, Alex Chandra-something," Asha said as she tried a piece of tandoori chicken. "He gave me and Alok an invitation. I just came to get a look at Nikhil. He's gorgeous, don't you think?"

Frank had spotted Nikhil deep in conversation with an older woman. She wore a black scarf over her head and dark sunglasses.

"Who's that he's talking to?" he asked, pointing the pair out to Asha. "She looks like a movie star, too."

"That's his mother," Asha said, laughing.

If Asha was a big fan of Nikhil, Joe figured she would know a lot about him. As they sat down at a round table set with six water glasses, he asked, "Why hasn't Nikhil had any starring roles yet?"

"I don't know," Asha said. She pushed the food on her plate around with a fork for a moment. "Maybe it's because he doesn't look like the typical Bollywood star, and no one wants to take a chance on him. He never talks about it to the media, but his father was English. He died when Nikhil was young."

Joe remembered the photo hidden in Nikhil's drawer. Frank was right; it didn't make sense that Nikhil would go to all the trouble and risk to frame Vijay for one starring role. But it might be worthwhile if this one role launched an entire career of starring roles.

As they finished eating, Vijay strolled over to their table. "You wanted to meet Alex Chandraswamy, didn't you?" He pointed to the dais at the front of the room, where a squat, round man in a baggy *kurtha* and heavy, yellow silk vest stood. His bald head glistened under the lights, and he shook hands vigorously with every person who came up to him.

Frank glanced at Asha. She seemed to be uncomfortable around Vijay, but when they got up to go meet Alex, she followed.

Chandraswamy was talking to Mahesh when Vijay and the Hardys approached him. Ignoring Vijay, Mahesh introduced Frank and Joe as Rajiv's American interns.

"Well, well," Chandraswamy said. "You'll have to stop by my office sometime. I'm starting a new film next week. We can always use a couple of extra pairs of hands."

"Rajiv keeps us pretty busy," Frank said.

"So I've heard." Chandraswamy raised an eyebrow. "If he insists on working outside industry standards, he's going to wear everyone out. No one makes a film in two months in this town."

"Why not?" Joe asked.

"It's just not done that way. And because of him, I have to delay—"

He was interrupted by Mahesh jabbing him in the side and whispering something in his ear.

"I've seen enough," Frank said to Joe under his breath as Vijay introduced himself to Alex. "Unless you want more to eat, I'm out of here." Mahesh may have had an alibi for last night, he thought, but he sure was chummy with Rajiv's sworn enemy.

"Well, it's early," Asha said as they left the dais. "Would you two like to take a walk on the beach? The moon is very bright tonight, and you need to stroll along the sea at least once before you go back home."

"Great idea," Joe said, pulling Frank along. "We haven't had much time for sight-seeing."

"This is how commoners have their fun in this city," Asha said as they stepped out. "Maybe we should take a camel ride instead."

They walked along the water's edge, listening to the waves slapping against the sand. The air smelled fresh and green, like seaweed or cut grass.

Gradually they saw more and more people and the beach got noisier. Within a half mile of the hotel, there was a small fair going on. There were several brightly lit stalls from which fried snacks were being sold. The smell of cooking oil was strong. Asha bought a cone of newspaper filled with what looked like roasted peanuts. "They're called *channa dal,*" she said. "Dry lentils." She shared some with Frank and Joe.

Another vendor was selling sweet coconut water. With a ten-inch blade, he hacked the top off a green coconut, then bored a hole into it with a hand drill. He inserted a straw and held it out to Joe.

"No thanks," Joe said, shaking his head. "I'm stuffed."

"You have to try this," Asha insisted, indicating that they would buy three. "No one leaves Bombay without drinking fresh coconut water."

They each took a couple of gulps, and when they were done, the vendor took their shells and tossed them into a pile behind him.

Several camels, trotting along the water's edge, had tourists on their backs and guides running beside them. Frank stopped at a table of knickknacks and bought a small purse decorated with mirror work for his girlfriend, Callie. Joe couldn't decide what to buy for Vanessa, and finally, with Asha's help, picked out a big, speckled cowry shell.

Once they'd passed a carousel powered by two men feverishly turning a wooden hand crank, the beach grew quiet and almost deserted. Joe and

Asha walked ahead, near the water, while Frank hung back and watched the running lights on a fishing boat as it came in for the night.

"So what about that camel ride?" Frank heard Joe ask Asha.

Moments later he heard galloping behind them. He turned just in time to see a huge camel bearing down on him, its cloaked rider rising up in the stirrups and lifting his right hand to raise a heavy club over his head.

Chapter
10

FRANK DOVE ASIDE, managing to get his head and torso out of the way of the camel thundering toward him. But the animal's churning legs whacked his feet and spun him around like a pinwheel so he had to lie on the sand, gasping for breath. He jumped up to dodge the next pass, but the rider wasn't interested in him anymore.

Frank watched, helpless, as the camel tore after Joe and Asha. "Get down!" he shouted.

They ran down the beach, Joe holding Asha by the elbow. The rider raised his club again, and Frank saw Joe grab Asha to shield her with his body. Then he heard a sickening thud and, as the camel took off down the beach, he saw the two of them crumple to the sand.

Frank ran toward them. "Joe! Asha!" he yelled. Joe got up, but Asha wasn't moving.

"I grabbed her too late," Joe said. "He got her." He leaned over and brushed Asha's dark hair away from her face. She groaned.

"Oooh, my back," she said, sitting up slowly. She pulled the neck of her dress down over her shoulder. Joe held up his penlight and saw a square-shaped red welt on her shoulder blade. It was already starting to swell.

"Do you think you can walk back to the hotel?" Frank asked her. "I don't think anything's broken, but you should be checked out."

Asha stood up carefully and brushed herself off. "It's just a bruise. What did that idiot think he was doing? Acting in a movie or something?"

"That was no act," Joe said. "Hey, look at that." He pointed to an object bobbing on the waves close to shore. After pulling off his shoes, he waded into the surf and grabbed it. "It looks like the business end of a cricket bat," he said, returning with the heavy chunk of planed wood.

"A cricket bat?" Frank examined the eight-inch fragment. It was flat like a paddle and had broken fairly cleanly. The only thing that wasn't right was that it was hollowed out. "Cricket bats are made of solid wood," he said. "Just like baseball bats." He handed it back to Joe. "Let's take a closer look at this back at the hotel."

"Who would do something like this?" Asha asked.

"That's what I'd like to find out," Joe said, his jaw set in a hard line.

They started back to the hotel, stopping at a camel stand along the way. There was a man sitting on a bench with a couple of harnessed and saddled camels behind him. Frank described the cloaked rider and asked if anyone fitting that description had rented a camel.

The man shook his head slowly as he counted through a roll of bills. "My partner or I must be leading them. We do not let camels or their riders run amok, sir."

The walk back was long, and although Asha didn't complain, she held the arm on her injured side close to her chest. It was obvious she was hurting. He'd been suspicious of Mahesh before, but he couldn't believe he or anyone conspiring with him would attack Asha.

"Why does your cousin seem to hate Vijay so much?" he asked.

"Oh, Mahesh? He has never forgiven Vijay for what he did to me."

"What do you mean?"

"Mahesh has a very outdated sense of chivalry," Asha said, trying to smile through her pain. "He arranged for me to go out to dinner with Vijay on my last visit here. At the last minute, Vijay got a better offer from some actress. He stood me up and then had the nerve to show up at the restaurant where I was waiting for him."

"That's why Mahesh is so cold to him?" Joe asked.

"That's right. Don't tell him I told you, though. He thinks he's protecting my honor by not mentioning it." As they passed the concession stands again, they could see the lights of the hotel in the distance.

"Mahesh is always looking out for me," Asha continued. "Now he's convinced I should move back to India and become a movie star." She laughed. "He claims it's a sure thing, but I think I'll keep my quiet life, especially after this."

When they reached the hotel, the party was still in full swing. They ran into Mahesh, who was out of breath and slightly frazzled.

"Have you seen Alok?" Mahesh said. "The last time I saw him, he was chatting up some young starlet. I wanted him to meet Alex, not actresses. He's never going to establish a network if he keeps this up."

He noticed Asha looking pale and ready to drop. "Are you sick, dear?" he asked. "I told you not to eat any food from vendors on the beach."

"A guy on a camel attacked us on the beach," Frank said. "Asha took a pretty good whack. I think she should see a doctor."

"Forget it," she said. "I'm just a little sore. Nothing a hot bath won't cure."

Leaving Mahesh in charge of Asha, the Hardys jogged back down the beach in the direction of the camel and its mysterious rider.

Joe made out a large shadow coming toward them in the darkness. It looked like a camel, but it wasn't galloping. It continued at a leisurely pace, and gradually the shape of a small boy materialized next to it. He was leading the camel by a ragged harness.

"Hey," Joe said, stopping the boy. "Where did you find that camel?"

The boy looked frightened and took a step backward, nearly bumping into the animal.

"Did you find the camel?" Frank asked. Maybe the kid didn't understand English.

The boy shook his head. "I am returning it. A man back there gave me five rupees to bring it back."

"Where did he go?" Frank asked.

The boy pointed to a pier farther up the beach.

"Did you get a look at him?" Joe asked.

The boy shook his head. "His face, it was covered behind the, the ..." The boy searched for the right word and made a motion around his face.

"A hood? A scarf?" Frank asked.

The boy nodded. "Yes, a scarf. And a red turban."

Joe grabbed Frank's shoulder. "Come on," he said, and they took off down the beach again. In a few minutes they came to a small marina. Wooden platforms with rusty oil drums lashed under them as floats formed a makeshift dock.

Several motorboats were moored in the slips. A weathered shack stood at the foot of the dock, where thick, barnacle-encrusted pilings connected it to the beach. There didn't seem to be anyone around.

"I wonder what's farther up the beach?" Joe said.

"It doesn't look like we can continue on foot," Frank said. Juhu Beach seemed to end here, with a large jetty sticking out on the other side of the docks. The water lapped gently against the jetty, and the wooden docks creaked with each swell of the ocean.

"You fellows," a voice said. A man in shorts and a white shirt popped out of the tiny hut onto the moon-bright sand. "I'm Ali. Would you like to rent one of my boats? Only twenty-five rupees an hour, plus petrol, of course."

"Actually, we're looking for a friend of ours," Joe said. "Did someone rent a boat in the last twenty minutes or so?"

"A man was here," Ali said. "But he didn't rent one of my boats. He had his own, and it was a fast one, too. He just took off, like that." Ali snapped his fingers.

"Which direction?" Frank asked.

"Where you just came from, very fast."

Joe looked at Frank. "The guy's long gone by now."

"Right," Frank said. "If it was someone from

the party, he could have bypassed us on the water and be back there already."

"What was he wearing?" Joe asked.

"So many questions," Ali said. "I don't know, some sort of cape or something, maybe a turban. Now, do you want to rent one of my boats or not?"

"No thanks," Joe said. "Maybe some other time, during the day."

"Sure, sure," Ali said with a dismissive wave of his hand. "That's what they all say."

Back at the hotel the ballroom was still packed, and there was no sign of the *mahurat* ending any time soon. The Hardys ran into Nikhil, who was dressed in expensive-looking linen pants and a white shirt.

"Having a good time?" he asked.

"Oh, sure, we've having a ball," Joe said.

"Did you find that on the beach?" Nikhil asked, pointing to the piece of wood that Joe was still carrying.

"Floating in the water, actually," Frank replied. There was plenty of eating and drinking still going on around them, with loud music and dancing in an adjoining room.

"You know, if you were looking for a souvenir, you could get a nice new bat for very cheap," Nikhil joked. "I understand Americans don't play cricket."

"No, we've got baseball," Joe said. "A much more interesting game."

"Come on, Joe," Frank said. "Let's call it a night." They headed for the exit, pausing only long enough for Joe to grab a couple of freshly made *samosas* for the road.

Out in the parking lot, they found out Sachin had gone home. He'd left a note with one of the other drivers, suggesting they take a scooter as far as Bandra and then get a taxi to Malabar Hill, since scooters were restricted to certain neighborhoods.

"Sounds like fun," Joe said. "But what's a scooter?"

Frank pointed to a bunch of small black cabs on three wheels clustered around the entrance of the hotel driveway. With their bright yellow roofs, the scooters looked like large covered tricycles with motors.

They went over and squeezed into the narrow backseat of the first one in line and told the driver their destination. He sat in the front, steering and braking with handlebars.

Once they got going, Frank said, "Every time we hit a bump I feel like we're going to tip over or I'm going to fall out."

"Well, at least it's more interesting than a taxi," Joe said.

Frank took the chunk of wood from Joe. "If you were a terrorist and wanted to smuggle explosives into the country, how would you do it?" he asked.

"I'd need a good hiding place," Joe replied. "Semtex is hard to detect—it won't set off metal detectors, and police dogs have a tough time smelling it—but I'd still want it to be well hidden, in case I got stopped in a random search."

Frank held up the end of the bat. "How about a hollowed-out cricket bat?"

"You're not serious," Joe said. "Do you really think Vijay's involved in some sort of terrorist operation?"

"No." Frank slapped his hand on the wood. "I agree with Mahesh on that one. Vijay's not the type, but I'd say someone in Rajiv's production is."

"Then this could go way beyond sabotage," Joe said.

Frank nodded and looked out the side of the scooter. He watched as a black sedan with tinted windows tried to pass them. The car was coming closer—a little too close, as far as Frank was concerned.

The driver noticed, too, speeding up and hugging the far shoulder of the road. Then Frank heard the sedan downshift and it shot ahead, veering sharply into their lane.

"Hang on," Frank shouted as the scooter driver squeezed both handbrakes hard. The big tricycle's wheels locked, and it spun out of control, rolling off the road and bouncing violently end over end.

Chapter

11

FRANK AND JOE BOUNCED off the windows, the
roof, and the seats of the scooter. Joe was wondering if they would ever stop flipping when the
scooter nose-dived into the pavement one more
time, then rebounded and slid to a stop on its
roof.

Joe felt like a contortionist. He was upside
down, the back of his neck and shoulders taking
all his weight. He felt Frank stirring next to him,
and he could see the driver, who didn't look
good. A trickle of blood ran down the man's
forehead, and he was obviously unconscious.

"How're you doing?" he heard Frank ask.

"I think I'm all right," Joe said, trying to turn
himself. He heard Frank's door pop open and
then saw his brother do a back somersault onto

the road. Joe forced his door open and tried the same thing but abruptly found himself falling.

Frank heard a splash and ran around the scooter to see what had happened. He found Joe sprawled in a drainage ditch.

"This is nasty," Joe said. "I think I landed in a pile of old mango peels or something."

"Come on, let's help the driver," Frank said, giving Joe a hand out of the ditch.

A couple of bystanders had arrived and were about to pull the driver from under the scooter by his shoulders. Frank stopped them. He didn't want to aggravate the man's injuries, and he could already hear the wailing siren of an ambulance on the way.

When the police showed up, the witnesses couldn't tell them any more than Frank and Joe could. They'd seen a black sedan with tinted windows run the scooter off the road. No one had seen the driver or the license plate.

The Hardys retrieved the piece of cricket bat and made sure their driver would be okay. He regained consciousness and seemed to have suffered a broken ankle and a gash on his scalp. Then they caught a regular cab and headed back to Rajiv's.

"I feel that we're as much of a target as Rajiv's film now," Joe said, examining his wet, smelly shirt.

"Oh, really, Joe?" Frank said. "Are you sure you didn't catch a dose of Rajiv's paranoia?"

"If this is paranoia," Joe replied, "you can lock me up right now, because I'm ready for a rubber room."

Frank smiled and said, "No, you're not, you're ready for a shower. You smell like rotten mango."

"Seriously, though," Joe said, ignoring his brother's comment, "they're onto us now, and it's got to be somebody close to the production."

Back at the house the Hardys were careful not to wake up Sachin and Rajiv. As soon as Joe got cleaned up and dressed, he was his old self again—ready for action.

"Hey, Frank," he said, pulling on a black T-shirt. "Are you caught up on your sleep?"

"What do you have in mind?"

"I've got an idea on how to catch these guys."

"Well, let's hear it," Frank said.

Joe unpacked their video camera. "This little baby is going to be our witness," he said. "Almost all the clues we have—the marble globe, the knife, the beard, the red turban—come from our prop room."

Frank figured out right away what Joe had in mind. "So we plant the camera in the room to see if we can catch the saboteurs planning their next move," he said.

"Right. Let's hit the road." Joe tossed Frank one set of moped keys.

It was well after midnight when Frank and Joe

padded quietly into the garage behind the house and wheeled the mopeds down the driveway and onto the street. Once they were far enough from the house, they fired the bikes to life and took off down Marine Drive.

Traffic was sparse, so they could ride close together, flashing through pools of greenish light thrown down by the streetlamps. They followed the ocean for a while, passing rows of palms and boxy condominiums. Joe followed Frank down the narrow alley leading to the palace. Tall buildings rose up on both sides of them, seeming to meet the night sky above, and then the alley opened up at the intersection where the maharaja's palace faced the old textile factory.

They stashed the mopeds down the street and moved back along the outer wall, careful to stay in the shadows where no one in the factory huts across the street could see them.

"How high do you think the wall is?" Joe whispered.

"Ten, twelve feet maybe. Here, you go first." Frank stood with his back to the wall and crouched down, lacing his fingers together to make a step up for Joe.

Joe backed up a few steps and got a running start, stepping into Frank's hand stirrup and vaulting up the wall. He grabbed the top edge and pulled himself up. He could see the guard asleep in his booth.

"All clear," he said.

Frank tossed the video camera case up to Joe, then gave himself a running start and jumped, grabbing Joe's hand and scrambling to the top. They dropped silently down into the courtyard. It took Joe only a few seconds to jimmy the front doors. Their biggest worry was getting them open without waking up the guard.

They each grasped one of the cast-iron rings that served as both doorknob and knocker and pulled slowly, their faces tense as the heavy wooden doors creaked on their hinges.

Once safely in, Joe led the way, staying close to the walls. They crept through the Hall of Public Audiences. Shafts of blue moonlight shining through the high windows spotlighted the guru's chair and the pillows surrounding it. With the set still in place, Frank felt as if they were breaking into Ram Jagannath's actual headquarters.

They followed the long hall down to the prop room, pausing at the entrance to make sure no one was around.

"Keep a lookout down here," Joe said. He had the camera in one hand and his pocket flashlight in the other. He found the spiral staircase and climbed cautiously up to the balcony, remembering what had happened to Frank.

After crouching down behind the stone screens, he searched for Frank. It was too dark to see him. The video camera had its own built-in spotlight, but to turn it on would be as good as not hiding the camera—anyone in the prop room would see the light shining through the screens.

"Frank," he said, "can you hear me?"

"Loud and clear," came the reply.

"Find a light you can turn on down there," Joe said. He heard Frank bump into something and grumble under his breath. Then he saw the slim beam of Frank's penlight play across the marble floor.

"There's a lamp on Alok's desk," Frank said.

Joe put the camera on the floor and aimed it down through the screen. "Now move the panel, will you?"

Frank folded back one of the partitions of the wooden panel separating Alok's desk from the rest of the prop room. "How's that?" he called up to Joe.

"Perfect." Joe pushed the Record button and the tiny video screen lit up. He zoomed in and then back. The picture was grainy, as though he were taping through a light snowstorm, but with the camera in just the right place, he could cover the entire row of prop shelves, the counter with the Styrofoam heads, and some of the costume racks. Leaving the camera running, Joe crept back downstairs.

"How long can it record?" Frank asked.

"I put the camera on its slowest tape speed," Joe said. "The picture won't be that clear, but we should get eight hours out of it." He glanced at his watch. "That'll cover the rest of the night until the shoot starts tomorrow."

"Nice going," Frank said. "Maybe we'll catch that 'ghost' that knocked me over the head two days ago."

"While we're here, are you up for searching more dressing rooms?" Joe asked.

"Let's not push our luck," Frank said. "That guard could come around anytime."

"Come on, he's sleeping like a baby."

Before Frank could say anything, Joe clicked off the lamp on Alok's desk and strode away toward the atrium.

When they came to the hall of dressing rooms, Joe searched for Kamala's gold star; it was his marker. He opened the door next to it and panned across it with his light, holding it on a coatrack where a set of plain beige robes hung. "Vijay's room," he said, shutting the door. He knew the next one was Nikhil's, so he passed it up. "Been there, done that," he said to Frank.

Joe slipped into the fourth door down the hall, motioning for Frank to follow. "Now this is more interesting," he said after he'd switched on the overhead light.

The room itself was tidy, but several combs and brushes, as well as a forest of bottles of aftershave and talcum powder, cluttered the top of the dresser. "Tariq's room," Frank said. He picked up a jar labeled Mustache Wax. Putting that down, he unfolded a map of Pune, a city southeast of Bombay.

"Shhh!" Joe said, holding his index finger to his lips.

Frank froze. At first he couldn't hear anything, but then he made out the sound of footsteps coming along the hall outside. He reached back and flipped off the lights.

Frank and Joe stood in the dark as the footsteps grew louder. Without time to scramble for a hiding place, they could only stand still and hope whoever it was went on past.

The footsteps paused at the door, and Joe saw the beam of a flashlight filter in around the edges. He held his breath, willing himself to remain calm.

The light around the door disappeared, and the footsteps continued on, trailing off down the hall.

Frank turned the light back on. "That was close."

"I can deal with close," Joe said, going to Tariq's wardrobe and rummaging around. He held up Tariq's red turban for Frank to see.

Frank sifted through the clothes in Tariq's dresser. "Uh-oh."

"What is it?"

"It's a book," Frank answered, holding up a thick volume bound in worn, cracked leather. *The Wisdom of Ram Jagannath in His Own Words,*" he read aloud.

"Tariq takes his role seriously," Joe said. "Kamala already told me that."

"I don't think she meant this seriously." Frank had opened the cover of the book and read from the title page. " 'To my dear disciple Tariq Khan. May peace and love be with you always. Ram Jagannath.' "

"So Tariq was a follower of Jagannath?" Joe came over to read the inscription for himself. "No wonder he was so upset with Rajiv's portrayal of Jagannath."

"I think Tariq has some explaining to do," Frank said.

"He's not the only one," Joe said, holding the book up for Frank to see. "You see this picture of the guru? He's the same person in the picture I found in Nikhil's room."

Frank let out a low whistle. "Which means . . ."

"Nikhil is Ram Jagannath's son."

Chapter

12

JOE SNAPPED THE BOOK CLOSED and put it back where Frank had found it. "I think we should be here in the morning when Tariq shows up," he said. "He looks like the kind of guy who'd spill his guts after a few tough questions."

"No," Frank said. "We should hold off. We know Nikhil is meeting someone early Friday morning, and we already have the camera set up. Let's wait and see if we can get some hard evidence on videotape. Then we can confront both Tariq and Nikhil."

Frank looked at his watch. It was almost four in the morning. "Besides," he said, "as long as we're up, there's something else we should do."

"Oh, yeah?"

"We landed at the airport at four in the morning, right?" Frank said.

"Right."

Frank paused, listening for sounds out in the hallway. Satisfied, he continued. "Baggage handlers work in shifts. So, if someone bribed airline employees to put Semtex in Vijay's suitcase, then they had to be on duty when our flight arrived." Frank held up his watch. "If we get to the airport now, we may be able to find those handlers, or at least ask who might be willing to take a bribe."

"Let's do it," Joe said.

The Hardys retraced their steps out of the palace. In the courtyard they checked the guard's booth, but it was empty.

"Still making his rounds," Joe said.

Frank got in position and helped Joe up the wall. As Joe reached down to help Frank up they heard the front door of the palace creak open. "Come on, Frank," Joe whispered.

Frank ran and leaped for Joe's hand, reaching the top of the wall just as the guard, his heavy belt jingling with his baton and pistol holster, ambled out into the courtyard.

Frank and Joe dropped down on the other side, landing hard on the sidewalk. They sat with their backs to the wall for a moment. The guard didn't seem to have noticed anything unusual. Across the street all the factory huts were dark, and an old man lay sleeping out on the sidewalk, a small bundle of clothes under his head for a pillow.

Frank and Joe rode along the coast again until

they spotted the red blinking lights of the Sahar control tower. Using the minaret-shaped tower as a guide, they turned inland, weaving through a maze of narrow streets lined on both sides with cars and parked bicycles. The buzz of the mopeds' engines echoed off glass storefronts and stone walls, and after driving down an alley, they would look up and adjust their course based on where the tower was.

When they got to Sahar, the arrivals terminal was crowded, just as it had been the morning they landed. Cabs and private cars packed the drive, and passengers, laden with bags or following porters in dark green uniforms, poured from the building. Joe pulled his bike up on the sidewalk and parked under a sign that had the name of their airline on it in both English and Hindi.

Frank started to walk through the double doors, but Joe stopped him. "Hold on," he said, "I have to get into character."

"What?"

"Just follow my lead," Joe said, patting his shirt pocket. "You have a pen I could borrow?"

Frank handed over his ballpoint.

Inside, Joe checked the monitor for incoming flight information, then walked confidently up to the ticket counter, where a man in a white dress shirt and blue tie stood stamping a stack of papers.

"I say there," Joe said, affecting a British accent and pretending to be very angry. "I say, what is your name?"

Startled, the man looked up.

Joe leaned forward to read the man's name tag. "I say, um, Rishi. Listen, we've just arrived on the flight from London, and our bags are absolutely ruined. It looks as though someone ran over them with a lorry!"

"I'm—I'm terribly sorry, sir," the ticket agent said. "But I have nothing to do with that."

"Nothing to do with it." Joe turned to Frank in mock astonishment. "You most certainly do. You are an employee of this airline, aren't you?"

"Yes. Yes, of course."

"Then I want you to go back in that little room of yours and look up the names of the luggage handlers on duty tonight." Joe snatched the pen from his pocket and rapped it on the counter. "I want those names, and I want them now."

Rishi held his hands up as if to say that there was nothing he could do. "But, sir," he said. "It's four-thirty in the morning. The desk manager will be here in just a few hours, and you can talk to him then."

"That's absurd," Frank said in his best British accent, slapping the counter with his palm. "Do you expect us to take our trampled bags to our hotel and then come all the way back here to straighten this out? I want those names this instant so I can report them to the airline."

Rishi stepped back from the counter slowly,

maintaining his dignity. "Yes, all right," he said. "I'll see what I can find. Just a moment, please." He went through the door behind the counter.

"Very convincing," Frank whispered to Joe. "Especially the accent."

Rishi returned with a handful of time cards. "There are a number of cards that have been punched for this morning," he said. "I don't have first names, but here are their last names. I hope that will be sufficient for you to make your complaint."

"I believe it will," Joe said, making a big production of writing the names down. "You've been more than helpful. Thank you very much, sir."

"Okay," Joe said as they left the ticket counter. "Now all we've got to do is find one of these guys and start him talking."

The Hardys hung around for a few minutes while the terminal cleared out. When no one seemed to be watching, Joe walked casually over to a door marked Airline Employees Only. The door was locked, but it looked like an easy target. As Frank shielded him, pretending to read a tourist brochure he'd picked up, Joe slipped a credit card between the door frame and door and worked it up and down. Within seconds he freed the latch.

Inside, Frank saw that it was a lounge area with stairs along the back wall leading down to the field outside. Plastic chairs in the colors of the airline surrounded round, Formica-topped tables, and rows of steel lockers lined one wall. The room was empty.

"Look," Joe whispered, pointing to the lockers. Each locker had an old, yellowed piece of tape across it, on which was scrawled an employee's name.

Joe scanned the names on his list, comparing them to the lockers. *Mahanty* was the first match he found. "Keep a lookout," he said to Frank, going to work with his lock pick this time.

The padlock popped, and Joe pulled out the contents of the locker—a pair of rope sandals, an incense candle with a small brass burner, and a stack of business magazines. "Nothing," Joe said.

As Frank stood watch by the door, Joe picked another locker marked *Singh,* than another with the name *Choudhury* written on the frayed tape. On the fourth match, marked *Rao,* Joe opened the locker, rummaged around for a few seconds, and said, "Bingo."

"What is it?" Frank asked, coming over.

Joe took the pen from his pocket and used it to pick up an expensive-looking maroon silk dress shirt with the initials *VT* monogrammed on the pocket.

"*VT* for Vijay Tate," Joe said. "We might get some prints off this."

Frank could see an identical shirt—except the color was royal blue—stuffed in the bottom of the locker, along with a pair of fancy leather tassel loafers.

"It looks like he had to make room in Vijay's bag for the explosives," Frank said.

"So he took out a few items," Joe said. "Then he made the mistake of trying to hold on to them. But how would whoever framed Vijay know his bag would get searched?"

"Easy," Frank said. "They just called in a tip to airport security. That way, everyone's bags would have to be searched."

"Right," Joe said. "Then when Sachin didn't make it in to pick up Vijay's bag, it just took the police a little extra time to find it and trace it to him."

"Now the question is, who bribed the baggage handler to switch the bags?" Frank said.

"Let's go have a little chat with Mr. Rao," Joe said with a quick gesture to the locker.

"I think it's time to call Lieutenant Bedi," Frank said. "Even if we haven't caught the saboteurs yet, they'll have to drop the charges against Vijay, and Rajiv won't have to shut down the production."

Frank left to make the phone call, leaving Joe meditating next to the bag. Joe couldn't let go of the thought that whoever was behind the attempt to frame Vijay was up to something even more serious than trying to stop Rajiv's filming. He could only hope that Detective Bedi could get the baggage handler to give up the names of whoever was behind the bag switch. That information should really lead somewhere. Until then, he knew who he'd be watching on the set.

But what good was this, Joe thought, just sitting around when the case was starting to heat up? Deciding to go find Rao, Joe got up and went down the stairs leading to the runway. He opened the door, and the roar of jet engines was deafening. As he stepped out on the field, he could see a huge airliner gradually climbing skyward from a nearby runway.

Joe clapped his hands over his ears as he walked toward a parked jumbo jet. Workers in blue coveralls were cranking the jetway back from the cabin of the plane—it had obviously recently finished unloading—as a tanker truck pumped fuel into its wings. A conveyor belt ran from the runway up into the building.

Joe went up to a man who was standing at the open door of the fuel truck.

"I'm looking for someone named Rao," he shouted over the din.

The man pulled up one ear of his headset so he could hear. "Eh?" he said.

"I'm looking for Rao."

The man gestured to the open belly of the plane at the next gate.

As Joe headed toward the other plane's cargo hold, he saw a man swing out of it and drop to the ground, not even bothering with the ladder.

"Hey, Rao!" Joe shouted.

The man sprinted straight for the conveyor belt and Joe followed, trying to cut him off. Rao made it to the belt first and belly flopped onto it. Diving after him, Joe hung on tight as the conveyor carried them up two stories off the runway toward a hole high in the wall of the terminal building.

Chapter

13

JOE SCRAMBLED UP the conveyor belt after Rao, grabbing him by the ankle. The baggage handler kicked back and almost knocked Joe off.

They were easily thirty feet above the concrete now, and as Rao disappeared into the building, Joe had a funny thought: he was about to be punished for the way he'd treated the front desk clerk earlier. He was also about to find out how luggage could get damaged on its way from the plane to the baggage carousel.

He ducked under the heavy flaps of rubber hanging over the belt, and suddenly he was inside a dark tunnel. The belt rattled like marbles in a coffee can. Inching forward on his hands and knees, Joe thought he felt something ahead of him. Was it Rao's shoe?

The belt changed direction suddenly, and Joe fell over on his side. More rubber flaps hanging from the ceiling fluttered along the length of his body.

The belt swerved again and Joe felt himself sliding down a chute. Then the darkness exploded into bright light and he slammed onto the baggage carousel, landing right on top of Rao.

Pushing Joe aside, Rao struggled to stand up on the revolving carousel. He got his balance for a second, then fell off, hitting the tiled floor of the baggage claim area. As Rao got up, Joe leaped off the carousel and tackled him. He got the baggage handler in a half nelson and wrenched his arm behind his back.

"Now," Joe said, catching his breath, "I want to know who paid you to plant Semtex in Vijay Tate's suitcase."

Joe felt someone tapping his shoulder. He turned to see Detective Bedi standing over him, looking rumpled and angry.

"We'll take it from here, if you don't mind," Bedi said. "I want to know what's going on."

Joe released the baggage handler and two police officers took over, locking handcuffs on the man. Another officer walked over from the employee lounge, carefully carrying Vijay's shirts and shoes.

"They were right where he said they would be," the officer said, nodding toward Frank.

Lieutenant Bedi pointed his right index finger at Joe's chest. "Your brother has explained your theories to me," he said. "And I'm going to take this man in for questioning. But I want to know why you decided to go after him on your own."

Joe just shrugged. What could he say?

"Well," Bedi said, stepping back and addressing both Hardys. "I'm going to check up on the two of you. My suggestion is that you stick to learning about movies and stay clear of this investigation. We don't appreciate you meddling in police business. Now get out of here," he said, his expression turning to an artificial smile, "and, of course, enjoy the rest of your stay in India."

Joe just stared back at the detective, but Frank came over and grabbed his brother's arm. "Come on, Joe," he said.

Outside the terminal, the sky was streaks of red and purple as the sun was rising. "How much did you tell him?" Joe asked as they climbed on their mopeds.

"Not much," Frank replied. "Just enough to get Vijay off the hook. I don't want them to shut down the production until we're sure how many people are involved. And I asked Bedi not to tell Rajiv that we were out here."

'He agreed to that?"

"I'm sure he'll be happy to take all the credit for himself," Frank replied with a smile.

Joe checked his watch. "It's been a long night. I could use a little sleep before we go back to the set."

* * *

Frank and Joe arrived at the palace just after noon, when everyone was breaking for lunch.

Mahesh greeted the Hardys at the doors to the Hall of Public Audiences and walked with them over to the caterer's table. "Stayed up late at the party last night, eh?" he said.

"You could say that," Joe said. "How's Asha doing?"

"It's a bad bruise, but she will be fine. I can't believe what happened to her, though. The world is just becoming a crazy place."

Frank noticed Vijay laughing with Kamala. "It looks like our stars are in good moods today," he said.

Mahesh frowned. "Yes. Vijay received some positive news this morning. The police discovered that someone bribed a baggage handler to place the explosives in his bag."

Joe looked over the food table for his new favorite food—*samosas*. "Did the police happen to say who it was who offered the bribe?" he asked.

"No," Mahesh replied. "According to Vijay, the baggage handler didn't give the police a name. He could only describe the fellow. Said he had a thick beard and wore sunglasses and a red turban. That was it."

"Well, at least Vijay doesn't have to worry about prison anymore," Frank said.

Mahesh looked over at Vijay disdainfully. "That's true, but he should be worrying about who tried to send him there." Mahesh put down his plate. "I have plenty of work for the two of you this afternoon," he said. "Alok and I are planning the scene where Jagannath's followers bomb the rival ashram."

"Excellent," Joe said. "I was looking forward to seeing some stunt work."

"Come take a look," Mahesh said, leading Frank and Joe over to where Alok and six or eight other crew members were fitting together two fake walls hung with long drapes.

"They're designed to come apart," Joe said.

"Exactly," Mahesh said. "This set assembles and disassembles quite easily, so we can move it outside when the time comes to shoot the actual stunt."

Frank felt the curtains. They were heavy like tapestries, and they covered the entire length of the ashram walls.

"This is supposed to be the meditation room at the rival ashram," Mahesh explained.

"What's the stunt?" Joe asked.

"When the bomb goes off," Mahesh said, waving his arms upward, "fire rushes up the curtains. The members of the ashram, played by extras and stunt doubles, of course, run out in a panic, ducking under a wall of flame."

"Wow," Frank said. "Sounds dangerous."

"We've done lots of planning. And besides, the local fire brigade will be with us, just in case the flames do get out of control." Mahesh excused himself to address a question from one of the crew.

"Everyone's out here for lunch," Joe whispered to Frank. "I'm going to see what we got on tape last night."

"Okay," Frank said. "I'll go check in with Sachin and Rajiv."

Joe took off down the hall toward the prop room. After making sure no one was around, he took out his flashlight and crept up the spiral staircase to the balcony.

The camera was there, just as he'd left it. Sitting behind the screens, he rewound the tape and then pressed Playback. First he saw Frank moving jerkily on the grainy film. Then he saw himself come into the picture and start talking with his brother. Then he turned out the light on Alok's desk and they both left.

Joe punched the Fast Forward button and watched as several hours of darkness passed by within the space of a few minutes. It ended with the digital readout indicating 7:07 A.M. when Alok and Mahesh came in, turned on the lights, and got to work.

He was disappointed but not ready to give up. He rewound the tape and set the camera timer to start taping at ten o'clock that night. That would cover the prop room until six the next morning. All he had to worry about was the battery pack running out of juice.

On his way back to the set, Joe saw Tariq turn

toward the dressing rooms carrying a plate over-flowing with food. This was his chance to corner him, whether Frank liked it or not.

Joe tiptoed behind the waddling old actor. After Tariq entered his dressing room, Joe waited a few minutes to let him settle in with his feast.

When he figured Tariq was nice and relaxed, Joe burst into the room—catching the actor with his mouth full—and slammed the door behind him.

Tariq choked in surprise. "What!" he sputtered, spilling food on himself and his dressing table. "What is the meaning of this intrusion?"

"Why did you kept your association with Ram Jagannath a secret?" Joe asked.

Tariq reddened. "What are you talking about?"

Joe marched over to Tariq's dresser and pulled out the book. "This is what I'm talking about," he said.

"How did you find that? What were you doing in this room? You have no right—"

"I was looking for evidence to prove who's been sabotaging this film," he said.

Tariq stood up so fast that he knocked his chair over. "You're supposed to be a film student. Who's paying you to snoop around like this?"

Joe realized he'd blown his cover. As he looked at Tariq—standing there with his jowls shaking in indignation and his tunic splattered with bits of food—he also realized the old actor was just too pathetic to be involved in any kind of sinister plot. The role of Ram Jagannath was probably the best one he had landed in a long time.

Joe had to back up and cover his tracks. "Okay, Tariq," he said. "I'll make a deal with you. You're right, I'm not on an internship for film school. My brother and I are investigators working for Rajiv."

Joe picked up Tariq's chair for him, and the old actor plopped back down in resignation. "If you can convince me that you were a perfectly innocent follower of Jagannath, then I won't tell anyone about it, and you won't tell anyone what my brother and I are really doing here."

Tariq took a deep breath. "I should have known someone would find out." He brushed a few blobs of food off his clothing as he spoke. "I met Ram Jagannath about ten years ago when I was in Pune. My career was a mess. I'd been in one flop after another. I had terrible money problems. So, finally I went out of town to recover for a while. Jagannath had just started his sermons, and I was captivated. He was very charismatic, you know.

"After the bombing, when I discovered his real identity, I was devastated. I kept this book, though, just to remind myself that he wasn't a complete fraud. He may have smuggled explosives and made money from other people's suffering, but he did bring peace to me and many others."

"So when you heard Rajiv was making a film based on his life, you signed on," Joe said.

"Yes. I don't agree with how Rajiv is presenting Jagannath, but with this part I can at least have some control over how people will see him."

Tariq sounded sincere, and Joe was in a hurry to get out of there. He paused at the door. "Remember our deal," he said, and turned to leave. He hoped he wasn't making a mistake by trusting Tariq.

In the Hall of Public Audiences the set of the rival ashram was almost complete, its curtained walls surrounding a carpeted platform. Meditation mats and pillows covered in gold- and copper-colored satin littered the set.

Rajiv had cornered Frank on the far side of the room and was shaking his clipboard in his face. "The good news we got about Vijay this morning came no thanks to you and your brother. I hope you had a fine time at the party last night."

"I think we're making progress," Frank said, making an effort to hold his tongue.

"I have half a mind to send you boys back to your father," Rajiv said. "It looks like our local police will soon have plenty of news to leak to the press, all at my expense."

Frank was about to answer when he heard a loud whooshing noise, like the sound of a giant blowtorch being lit. All the air seemed to be sucked out of the room in an instant, and Alok came running from behind the curtained walls shouting, "Fire! Everyone get out now!"

Chapter

14

MOST OF THE CAST AND CREW ran for the door, pushing and shouting. Flames streaked up one of the curtains, and thick black smoke laced with burning embers and pieces of cloth boiled toward the arched ceiling.

Frank rushed to the platform and, with the help of Mahesh and a few crew members, tore the burning curtain from its wall. It fell in a heap at their feet. Swinging a pillow in each hand, Mahesh beat wildly at the flaming tapestry, but the pillows caught fire, too.

"Drop them!" Frank shouted.

Mahesh threw the pillows into the fire as Frank ripped another of the curtains down and tossed it over the pile like a net. Frank and Mahesh ran to grab fire extinguishers, and two crew members followed.

Frank's quick move with the curtains had half-smothered the flames, and the foam from the extinguishers did the rest.

Frank wiped the sweat from his forehead with the tail of his shirt. "Man, that was close," he said.

"I don't see how that could have happened," Mahesh said. He lifted the corner of the curtain and stomped out the last few smoldering embers.

"Nice move," Vijay said, clapping Frank on the back. "Very professional."

But Rajiv didn't seem so happy. Staring up at the smoke-stained ceiling in disbelief, he let out a groan. "What a mess. What will the maharaja say?" he said. "This whole production is a disaster." He threw his clipboard to the floor. "Sachin, call the fire department. I want to know why this happened. Sachin? Where are you?"

Some of the extras who'd fled out the door were now quietly making their way back. Frank looked around for Sachin, finally spotting him crouching behind some lighting equipment.

"Get over here, Sachin," Rajiv bellowed. "The fire's out now."

Rajiv announced that the set was closed for the rest of the day and sat down with his head in his hands to wait for the local firefighters.

A few minutes later Joe returned from his confrontation with Tariq. "It looks like a bomb went off in here," he said, surveying the damage as several crew members cranked open the casement windows to let in fresh air.

"I think it did," Frank said. "Only it was supposed to be a stunt. Somebody must have set it off early before anybody was ready, and it blew out of control."

When the fire chief arrived, he questioned Rajiv and Mahesh, then poked around for a while, putting samples in plastic bags for later testing. He said it could be days or even weeks before he had any firm results.

That evening Rajiv locked himself in his study, refusing to come out for dinner.

"I don't think Rajiv can take much more of this," Sachin said, pouring himself a cup of tea after they'd eaten.

"Did he say anything to you?" Frank asked.

"He won't talk at all, but I know what he's thinking." Sachin sipped his tea. "If this film doesn't get made, he'll quit forever. It will be the end of his career."

"I guess that'll be a big disappointment for you, too," Joe said.

"Disappointment doesn't begin to describe it. I've been waiting five years for this. And it's not a question of money. I'm proud of working with Rajiv. I'll probably be finished in this business, too, if the film is canceled."

Sachin was pretty upset, and the Hardys decided it was time to excuse themselves and head upstairs.

"We don't have much time to wrap up this case before Rajiv calls it quits," Joe said after he'd closed the bedroom door behind him.

"Is that why you jumped all over Tariq today?"

"Give me a break, Frank. It wasn't such a big deal."

Frank looked out the window. "I hope not."

"Don't sweat it," Joe said, lying back on his bed and crossing his arms behind his head. "Nikhil's breakfast meeting is tomorrow, and my bet is that he picked up where his father left off in the explosives-smuggling business. He's going to meet his connection, and we're going to catch him at it."

Frank turned around. "Where was Nikhil today, anyway? I didn't see him on the set."

"I don't know," Joe said. "But he's only Vijay's stand-in and stunt double, so he doesn't have to be there all the time."

Although it was barely eight P.M., Frank climbed into bed, too. "How about setting that alarm for four-thirty?"

"Done." Joe set it and stuffed it under his pillow so they wouldn't wake up the rest of the house.

The Hardys had figured that getting up at four-thirty A.M. would give them plenty of time to check the videotape at the palace one last time before zeroing in on Nikhil at the Taj Mahal Hotel.

They scaled the wall easily. This time the guard wasn't asleep in his booth, so they assumed he was out making his rounds.

The palace smelled like smoke, and the burned ashram set sat like an ancient ruin in the shadows of the Hall of Audiences.

When they got to the prop room, Frank stood watch at the foot of the spiral staircase while Joe went up to check the camera.

Up on the balcony, Joe picked up the camera and punched the Rewind button. It whirred to life and the tape started spooling backward. When it clicked to a stop, Joe punched Play and waited.

The screen was black, the time notation on the tiny screen ticking ahead—10:30, 10:31, 10:32. Nothing. Joe fast-forwarded the tape, watching the time accelerate—11:45, 12:05, 1:20, 2:10. Still nothing.

Downstairs Frank kept watch. It was so quiet, he could hear the tape running through the camera above him.

Then he heard Joe whistle through his teeth.

"What is it?" Frank asked, looking up the spiral steps.

"Come on up," Joe whispered.

Frank found Joe crouching on the floor in the

dark, the video screen casting an eerie glow on his face.

Joe rewound the film a little. "Watch what happens at three-oh-two."

Frank knelt down and watched as the screen went from black to grainy white.

"Those are the lights coming on," Joe said. "Now take a look at this."

Frank saw a figure appear on the screen from the left, walk over to a costume rack, and pull some sort of tunic or coat off a hanger.

"The resolution is lousy," Frank said. "I can't tell who that is."

"Just wait."

The figure went over to the wig counter and walked down the line. He seemed to be trying on different false beards, but his back was to the camera. He then moved to the prop shelves and dug around, obviously looking for something in particular. To Frank the film looked like old footage of Bigfoot; there wasn't enough light, and he could hardly make out any details at that distance.

Then the figure turned and walked directly toward the camera.

"Alok," Frank said.

"Gotcha," Joe said to the figure on the screen.

"No," a voice said from the top of the stairs. "I've got *you*. Now freeze!"

It was the guard. He pulled out his snub-nosed

revolver and pointed it at Joe. "Give me the tape," he said.

"Okay, just stay calm. Don't shoot," Joe said, standing up and holding out the camera. At the last second he flipped on the camera's spotlight and flashed it in the guard's eyes. As the man straightened up, temporarily blinded, Frank charged into him, knocking him down the stairs. Joe heard the gun clatter across the prop room floor.

The two brothers were downstairs in a second, grabbing the guard and forcing him into the chair at Alok's desk.

"You're in this with Alok, aren't you?" Joe asked. He picked up the revolver and emptied out the bullets. "You and whoever else is sabotaging the film."

The guard shook his head. "I don't know what you're talking about," he muttered.

Frank pulled Alok's grappling hook from the prop shelf and untied the rope attached to it. "Here, Joe," he said. "Tie him up."

"Do you want to call Lieutenant Bedi?" Joe asked.

"No." Frank checked his watch. "We don't have time to deal with him now. Nikhil's meeting is in just over half an hour."

"Let me go and they'll give you as much money as you want," the guard said. "Name your price."

"Who?" Joe asked. "Alok and who else? Who's in on this?"

"Let me go first and I'll tell."

"Forget it. You're staying here and we're leaving."

Frank came out of Mahesh's office and said, "I just tried to call Rajiv, and there was no answer. He and Sachin must be on their way here already."

"Write them a note," Joe said. "Tell them that Alok is one of the saboteurs and that they should call Bedi immediately."

Frank hastily scribbled a note, dropped it on Mahesh's desk, and left with his brother.

Twenty minutes later the Hardys were parking their mopeds a block down the street from the Taj Mahal Hotel in the center of Bombay. The sun had already climbed over the tops of the buildings, and the street was teeming with vendors and people on their way to work.

The hotel had walls of polished white marble and five towering, gold-tipped spires that reached up to the sky. The brothers went in and found the restaurant just off the lobby. They found a table with a good view of both the door and the windows out onto the street, then sat down to wait.

After a few minutes Nikhil came in. He took a table by the window, pulled off his sunglasses, and put them in his shirt pocket as he sat down.

A waiter came by with menus.

"I'm starving," Joe said.

"Just order toast and tea and the check," Frank said. Just then he saw the tall woman Nikhil had been talking to at the party walk by the window and come into the restaurant.

"Oh, man," Joe said. "It's his mom. We just staked out Nikhil to catch him having breakfast with his mother."

"Let's wait and see what happens," Frank said.

The waiter came to take their order. Three minutes later he brought it and they paid, then ate their toast in silence, keeping an eye on Nikhil. Finally they saw him stand up, drop some money on the table, and kiss his mother on the cheek. He put on his sunglasses and strode briskly out of the restaurant and into the lobby.

"Here we go," Frank said.

Nikhil went out the back of the hotel and down a narrow street lined with cheap hotels.

"He must be meeting someone," Joe said.

Nikhil was taller than most of the people crowding the sidewalk, and the brothers stuck with him by following his light brown hair as it floated over the sea of heads around him. He turned down an alley and the Hardys followed.

They were between two hotels, and Frank could hear the clanking of dishes coming from the kitchens. Flies swarmed around piles of garbage lined up against the walls.

"Did you see where he went?" Joe whispered

when they were halfway down the alley. It was a dead end, which backed up to a mossy brick wall.

Just then Nikhil stepped out of a doorway. "Why are you two following me?" he asked.

Joe was about to explain when they heard an engine revving and turned to see the black sedan with tinted windows wheel into the alley, blocking their only path of escape.

Chapter

15

A BEARDED, MUSCULAR FIGURE stepped out of the car wearing the all-too-familiar red turban and sunglasses.

"Alok," Frank said. "We know it's you, and we know you're the one who tried to push us over the cliff."

The bearded man just grinned and reached into the car, pulling out a battle sword with a long, curving blade.

Alok ran his thumb down the tempered steel as he came forward. "See," he said. "No prop this time."

The Hardys stood with their backs to each other, ready to face off against both Alok and Nikhil. Frank crouched, reminding himself to stay low.

Joe had to make a split-second decision: help Frank or fight Nikhil. Hearing Alok charge behind him, he turned, telling himself it was his only choice—he had to expose his back.

Frank dodged out of the way as Alok brought the sword straight down, slicing through the air. The heavy blade clanged against the ground, scarring the bricks.

Joe felt something whistle past his right ear, and then saw a stone thump Alok in the chest. Joe heard him gasp as if he'd had the wind knocked out of him.

Nikhil rushed by. "Get him!" he yelled.

Alok turned and jumped onto the hood of the car. As Frank, Joe, and Nikhil edged toward him in a semicircle, he scrambled over the top of the sedan and escaped out the alley and down the street, carrying his sword with him.

Nikhil brushed the dirt from his hands and turned to Frank and Joe. "That was Alok?" he asked in amazement. "He was ready to kill us!"

"Don't think you can fool us with that little performance," Joe said. "You knew that was him all along."

Nikhil's face reddened with anger. "All I want is an explanation of why you were following me."

"We know who you are, too," Joe continued. "Ram Jagannath's son."

"Who told you that?"

"No one told us," Frank said. "We found your family picture."

"Great. And now you can sell the story to the highest bidder," Nikhil said.

"We're not journalists," Frank said. "Rajiv hired us to find out who's sabotaging his film."

"You think I'm part of some plot to ruin Rajiv?" Nikhil said. "That's ridiculous!"

"Maybe not after you just helped us," Frank said. "But we had our suspicions."

"There's nothing to be suspicious of," Nikhil said. "My father died when I was young, and my mother refuses to talk about him. I hoped doing this film would help me find out something about my father. I wouldn't think of sabotaging this production."

"So you're not working with any outsiders to ruin Rajiv's career?" Joe said.

"Of course not. I signed a deal with Alex Chandraswamy for his next picture, and I kept quiet about it because Rajiv hates him so much. That has nothing to do with sabotage."

Frank looked at Joe. "I take his word for it," he said. "Now let's go after Alok and hope he leads us to whoever else is involved."

Borrowing Nikhil's cell phone, Frank called Sachin at the set to get Alok's address. As he talked, the three of them edged past the black sedan and out into the sunny street. After a few minutes Frank clicked off the phone and handed it back to Nikhil.

"They gave me directions," Frank said as he and Joe jogged to their mopeds. There was no room for Nikhil, so he said he'd go to the set and remain there if they needed him. "Sachin says he and Rajiv just got to the palace and found the guard and the note. He'll tell Bedi to meet us at Alok's."

They left the busiest part of the city, weaving between cars and around pedestrians. Frank led the way as they cruised along the coast. Joe noted that the number of houses and apartment buildings was gradually thinning out. By the time Frank pulled over, there was almost nothing around, just miles of deserted beach and a couple of abandoned factories.

Joe was looking at a cluster of whitewashed shacks on the beach. "Is this it?" he asked.

They climbed over the guardrail and walked down the beach, staying just behind a row of sand dunes. When they got closer, Frank spotted a speedboat moored at a single-slip dock in front of the shacks. "This looks like it," he said.

The Hardys crept up to the nearest shanty, being careful to stay below the windows.

Joe found the door and opened it a crack. He peered inside. "Frank, in here," he whispered. He groped around in the dark, finally finding a light cord. When he pulled it, a single, naked lightbulb hanging from the center of the ceiling came on.

"My, my, my," Joe said. Wooden crates with shipping labels from England and Pakistan were stacked against the walls.

Frank pulled out his pocketknife and pried up the lid of the nearest crate. He tossed aside some paper packing first, then held up a cricket bat. It felt unusually light. "How much do you want to bet this is hollowed out, just like the one Asha was attacked with."

"No bet," Joe said. "It would be the perfect way to smuggle plastic explosive."

"That's right, Joe Hardy," Sachin said, standing in the doorway.

Startled, Frank dropped his pocketknife behind the crate.

"Sachin?" Joe said. "You're working with Alok?"

Sachin pulled a snub-nosed .38 from under his tunic and leveled it at the Hardys. "I got your note, you clever fellows," he said. "But, sorry, I seem to have neglected to call the police."

The gun looked exactly like the one the guard had, and Joe remembered that he'd taken the cartridges and dumped them outside the palace. As he took a step forward, Sachin pointed the pistol straight at him.

"I wouldn't," he ordered. "I reloaded it and used the first bullet on the guard. He won't be talking to anyone anymore."

The answer came to Frank in a flash. "You and Alok were both out of the country at the same time," he said. "You're the two Jagannath followers who tried to break him out of prison five years ago."

Alok appeared in the doorway, carrying a coil of rope and a knife. He said something to Sachin under his breath, and Sachin said, "Fine. Tie them up and then we'll get rid of them."

"When the escape attempt failed, Alok fled to Pakistan," Frank said. "Where did you go?"

Alok motioned for the brothers to sit on the floor. Holding the knife between his teeth, he quickly bound Frank's ankles and wrists and then moved to Joe.

"I just stayed in Bombay, waiting for the commotion to die down," Sachin said. "I was working in the film industry when I met Jagannath and saw no reason to quit that work."

Alok dragged Frank and Joe over to a wall and looped the rope around one of the exposed support beams. Then he patted them down, finding Joe's pocketknife.

"Smuggling was a very lucrative business for the ashram," Sachin said. "So Alok and I decided to go into business for ourselves. After all, I don't want to be Rajiv's slave for the rest of my life."

"Let's go," Alok said. "We have to prepare the boat."

"But why sabotage the film?" Frank asked as Sachin turned to follow Alok out the door.

Sachin adjusted his wire-rim glasses. "Renewed interest in Jagannath was the last thing we wanted. We couldn't risk the attention the movie would draw. Besides, Rajiv got him all wrong."

Sachin left, and the Hardys heard him bolt the door from the outside.

"We've got to get out of these ropes before they come back," Joe said.

Frank stretched out as far as he could from the wall. "I dropped my pocketknife behind this crate when Sachin came in," he said. Managing to knock the crate aside, he tried to reach the knife with his foot. "It's too far away."

"I'm going to try something," Joe said. "Keep your head down."

Using the toe of his left shoe, Joe pushed the heel of his right sneaker down and wiggled his foot free. Balancing the shoe on his foot, he thrust his legs up, propelling the sneaker toward the lightbulb overhead.

The bulb exploded, raining glass down on their heads. "There's a big piece close to you," Joe said, nodding toward a shard of glass about the size of a quarter.

Frank carefully brought the glass close with the edge of his shoe, then twisted at the waist and grasped it in his hands. Ignoring the pain in his wrists, he methodically cut at the ropes with the glass. Within several minutes he said, "Got it."

He hurried to untie Joe, and they went to the door.

"Locked," Joe said, glancing out the front window. "Quick, get down. They're coming back."

Chapter

16

FRANK AND JOE ducked down and heard Sachin's voice coming through the door as he unbolted the lock. "Give me the syringes," he said.

Alok said something unintelligible.

"Good," Sachin said. "This will knock them out for a nice, long time. By the time their bodies are found, there will be no trace of medication."

Sachin pushed the door open. Standing on either side of it, the Hardys took him and Alok by surprise. Frank grabbed Sachin, twisting his wrist and forcing him to the ground. The plastic syringe skittered across the floor.

Alok froze in the doorway, his broad shoulders blocking out the light. As he went for his knife, Joe pivoted from his hiding place beside the wall and thrust his knee into Alok's solar plexus. Alok doubled over, clutching his belly. Bending his knees for leverage, Joe smashed a right uppercut into Alok's jaw. He staggered back out onto the sand, arms flailing. Joe saw a trickle of blood run down from Alok's nose into his mustache.

"Enough!"

Joe turned to see Sachin lying on his back with Frank hovering over him, ready to throw a punch.

Sachin had managed to pull his gun. He pointed it up at Frank. "Get off me now," he said.

Outside, Alok pulled his knife. He beckoned Joe with the blade. "Come on out and play," he said with a sneer. Blood ran down his chin.

Sachin stood up, and as he looked away to find the syringe, Frank rushed for the door. "Get out," he shouted, pushing Joe ahead of him.

Sachin fired wildly, the bullet blowing a hole the size of a baseball into the wall just above the door. Frank pulled the door closed and bolted it, locking Sachin inside.

Now it was the two of them against Alok and his knife.

The Hardys stood on either side of Alok, circling around him as he jabbed at them with the dagger.

Joe feinted and Alok went for it.

When Alok thrust at Joe, Frank spun into a roundhouse kick. He heard the stuntman's ribs crack at the impact of his heel, and Alok collapsed in the sand, writhing in pain.

Joe picked up the knife. "Alok," he said, "if you even try to get up, I'm going to ask Frank to practice a few more of his kung fu moves on you."

Frank dove to the ground as three gunshots went off behind them in rapid succession. Joe dropped and rolled. He saw three bullet holes around the door handle of the shack.

"He's trying to shoot off the lock," Frank said.

One more shot ripped through the air, and the door swung open slowly.

Knowing that Sachin had used his six shots, Frank and Joe charged before he could reload. They quickly overpowered him and dragged him out onto the sand next to Alok.

"Hey, Sachin," Frank said. "Can we borrow your cell phone to call the cops?"

"Don't bother," Joe said, pointing over the dunes toward the road. Rajiv and Bedi, along with several uniformed officers, were approaching.

While two of the officers cuffed Sachin and took him away, another radioed for an ambulance for Alok. Meanwhile, Lieutenant Bedi lit into the Hardys.

"I thought I told you to stay out of this," he said.

"We told Sachin to call you," Frank replied, "but I guess he decided to ignore our message."

Bedi did not find that amusing. "You're lucky you weren't hurt."

"Oh, Lieutenant, leave them alone," Rajiv said. "They've been through enough already."

After Frank and Joe promised to stop at the station and give detailed statements, Bedi stalked off without a word.

Rajiv scowled as he watched officers put Sachin in the back of a car. "Sachin," he said. "I don't understand. He got beaten up, didn't he? Maybe Alok framed him, too."

"I don't think so," Frank said. "He definitely wanted to stop this movie. He and Alok were in it together. I think they were just bribing the guard to give them free access to the set."

"Yes, another very sad thing," Rajiv said, shaking his head. "That's how we knew where to find you. Mahesh found the guard's body in the prop room. We called the police immediately, and while Bedi was on the set, Nikhil rushed in and told us that you were going after Alok. We came here as fast as we could."

Frank and Joe walked up the beach with Rajiv to where they'd parked their mopeds.

"I'd like you two to take the day off tomorrow," Rajiv said. "You've earned it."

"Thanks," Joe said. "I guess we'll be getting a vacation out of this trip after all."

As it turned out, Rajiv gave everyone the day off. Frank and Joe met Asha, Mahesh, and Nikhil on the causeway to the Haji Ali Mosque. Together they crossed over and went down to sit on the wall between the sidewalk and the beach. Frank tossed bread crumbs to the seagulls circling overhead, and Joe munched on some freshly roasted *channa*.

"Funny how Sachin turned out to be such a good actor," Frank said.

"That's for sure," Joe said. "He pretended to be terrified of the cobra when he was the one who planted it. His only mistake was that he bought one that wasn't poisonous."

"But it must have been Alok who climbed up the trellis," Mahesh said, watching the colorful parade of characters walk by on the beach. "Now that I think about it, I remember him leaving while Vijay and I sat on the couch and watched that terrible movie."

"I just can't believe you thought Mahesh and I were involved," Nikhil said.

"Sachin and Alok did a great job covering their tracks," Frank said.

"They seemed to be the ones with the most to lose if the production got canceled," Joe added.

"So," Asha said as they slid off the wall and walked down to the water, "what happens now?"

"Actually," Nikhil said, "all the publicity is probably going to help the movie."

"Rajiv is finally going to open the set to writers and photographers," Mahesh said. "The film is news now, and that's going to attract a big audience when we finally finish it.''

"Three years from now, that is?" Joe said.

"No way," Mahesh said. "In a month. Rajiv hasn't changed his mind about the contracts. In fact, now that he knows the damage was the work of agents of Jagannath and not disgruntled actors, he's even more committed to defying the industry."

"What about Alex Chandraswamy?" Joe asked Nikhil.

"He'll wait. Rajiv knows I've signed with him now, so at least I don't have to worry about being found out. He also knows about my father. He thinks my mother and I should come forward with the story ourselves so that we have more control over what appears in the media."

"That makes sense," Frank said. "Especially with all the publicity the movie's getting."

Nikhil nodded, but he didn't look too happy.

"Don't worry," Asha said. "We'll figure out something over dinner tonight." She winked at Joe. "See, I get my date with a movie star, after all."

"Just don't stand her up," Mahesh joked. "Otherwise, I'll have to beat you senseless."

A group of schoolgirls dressed in blue-and-white uniforms, their hair braided and tied with blue ribbons, approached Nikhil with pens and open notebooks. They giggled as he signed each one and then passed them to Frank.

"He's a well-known movie star in America," Nikhil said to the girls. "This may be your last chance for an autograph."

Joe managed to keep a straight face as Frank blushed and signed the books. Satisfied, the girls took off.

"Their friends are going to be so jealous," Joe said, chuckling.

"Right," Frank said with a grin. "Except I signed your name. They'll all be bragging about how they got Joe Hardy's autograph—that is, until they figure out you're really nobody."

Frank and Joe's next case:

Frank Hardy has joined a Bayport fencing class, and although just a beginner, he's been selected to participate in a major tournament. But the competition is cutthroat—in more ways than one. He and his brother, Joe, who's coming along for the ride, will have to keep their wits *and* their swords sharp if they want to stay alive. One of Frank's top rivals vanishes, and the boys suspect kidnapping. Their search leads them to the castle estate of a wealthy industrialist, sponsor of an elite—and deadly—fencing team. Doing battle with saber and samurai sword, the Hardys make a sinister discovery that could turn a single grudge match into a fight to the death ... in *Blood Sport,* Case #117 in The Hardy Boys Casefiles™.

Christopher Pike presents....
a frighteningly fun new series for your younger brothers and sisters!

SPOOKSVILLE

The Secret Path 53725-3/$3.50
The Howling Ghost 53726-1/$3.50
The Haunted Cave 53727-X/$3.50
Aliens in the Sky 53728-8/$3.99
The Cold People 55064-0/$3.99
The Witch's Revenge 55065-9/$3.99
The Dark Corner 55066-7/$3.99
The Little People 55067-5/$3.99
The Wishing Stone 55068-3/$3.99
The Wicked Cat 55069-1/$3.99
The Deadly Past 55072-1/$3.99
The Hidden Beast 55073-X/$3.99
The Creature in the Teacher
00261-9/$3.99

A MINSTREL® BOOK

FEAR STREET® SAGA

Collector's Edition

Including
The Betrayal
The Secret
The Burning

R·L·STINE

Why do so many terrifying things happen on Fear Street? Discover the answer in this special collector's edition of the *Fear Street Saga* trilogy, something no Fear Street fan should be without.

Special bonus: the Fear Street family tree, featuring all those who lived—and died—under the curse of the Fears.

Coming in mid-October 1996

From Archway Paperbacks
Published by Pocket Books

POCKET
BOOKS